PRAISE FOR J.S. ARQUIN

★ ★ ★ ★ ★ "Divergent meets Hunger Games and then some. Could not put this one down.

★ ★ ★ ★ ★ "Writer in control of all. The story sweeps you along with it."

★ ★ ★ ★ ★ "More Please. After reading the prequel (Twist) I was hooked. Ascent was a great follow up and I can't wait for book two in the series to be released."

★ ★ ★ ★ ★ "Found this gem. A great read. Solid sci-fi. Looking forward to more by this author."

★ ★ ★ ★ ★ "The book is nonstop action and adventure."

★ ★ ★ ★ ★ "Like the Hunger Games, but better. I loved this book."

★ ★ ★ ★ ★ "Exciting and intriguing … a great read from beginning to end. Can't wait to read the next one."

Join J.S. Arquin's Reader Group for exclusive news and deals: www.arquinworlds.com

PEAK

BOOK THREE OF THE CRIMSON DUST CYCLE

J.S. ARQUIN

WORDS ON THE WIND, LLC

1

I surface in a cave, my consciousness swimming up through layers
of mist. My eyes are gummy, lashes stuck together with grit. I'm
lying on a narrow shelf of rock, cold seeping through the thin mattress,
streaks of glowing lichen illuminating deep crevices above me. There's
a pot of soup bubbling over a small fire, and shelves carved into the
rock hold containers of various shapes and sizes.

I try to open my eyes and find my right eye is stuck shut. I reach up
to wipe the sleep from my lashes and find thick bandages covering it.
The whole thing feels scabbed over. A dull ache throbs deep in my
socket.

I feel the sharp pain of Julius's warpknife slicing across my eyeball.

It all comes flooding back.

My crew infiltrated the Mesa and tried to decapitate the Guardian
offensive by assassinating the newly appointed governor, Julius
Carlyle. It all fell to pieces when Julius ambushed us instead. As I fled
through the tunnels with my crew of Outsiders, the Guardians picked
us off one by one.

I flinch, remembering my desperate duel against Julius. He toyed
with me, sinking the tip of his warpknife into my flesh again and again
—just as his brother Octav used to toy with me when we were students

together back in Merrimac, before I killed him in our final exam. My dad stepped between us, trying to protect me, and Julius plunged the warpknife through the center of his chest. I can feel my dad gasping in my arms, his hot blood soaking my hands.

Then Knott's cannon brought the ceiling of the cavern down, an avalanche of mud that pushed me and my dad out into the cold of the underground river. The river swept us away, shining like blood in the red light of my greicagin-sight, as if we were caught in the planet's arterial veins.

After a long time, we washed up on a stony river bank, where Jmini told me his scans could find no sign of living Outsiders: The Guardian's offensive had erased them from the scablands.

There I listened to the rattle of my dad's last breath.

Everything collapses down to his face, cold and pale on the bank of the river. My fault. My rockhead plan got my dad killed.

I roll over onto my side, my heart pounding, trapped by the jagged walls of my memories. I have to do something. Fix it somehow. I have to get out of here.

There's no sign of my armor or my warpknife, but they are not the only tricks up my sleeve.

"Jmini, are you awake?" I subvocalize carefully, letting the sound travel through the bones of my skull to reach the implant behind my ear.

Jmini "hmmms" like I'm interrupting his reading. "I've been awake for hours. You're the one who's been sleeping like a lump."

I exhale in relief. At least I'm not alone. Now I just have to figure out where I am.

I sense movement. The old hermit, Rust, strides across the cave in his ragged robe, muttering to himself.

"You might as well get comfortable. They probably think you're dead." Rust stops at the pot, stirring the bubbling broth with a long spoon. To my relief, there's no sign of the Rock Horror.

"Who thinks I'm dead?"

"Everyone, I imagine. You never checked in after your attack went sideways."

I swing my legs over the side of the pallet and sit up.

"I've got to get a message to them. Tell them I'm alive." I stop as what he's saying sinks in. "Wait. Back up. Who are we talking about? I thought everyone was dead."

"No, not dead. Just scattered. The Guardian offensive has driven the Outsiders deep underground."

"Ianna's alive?"

I blink back sudden tears. I thought everyone was gone. I thought I was alone for good this time.

"As far as I know. There's a lot of comm silence out there. People don't want to give away their positions."

"But you think she's alive?"

"I don't see why she wouldn't be. The Guardians are claiming victory, but I know the Outsiders. They're harder to kill than you think."

I push myself to my feet.

"I have to find her."

Rust turns from the soup to face me. His deep-set eyes have a faint metallic sheen to them, like the eyes of a Rock Horror. "Letting them think you're dead is the kindest thing you can do for them."

"Am I your prisoner, Rust?"

"Prisoner?" He rolls the word around like it tastes funny. "No, I wouldn't say that."

"If I'm not a prisoner, why did you take my warpknife and armor?"

"I took your gear so you wouldn't do anything stupid when you woke up. I'd hate to have to hurt you after I went to all the trouble of saving you."

"Saving me? You think you saved me? Saved me from what?"

He shrugs and tastes the soup. Grimacing, he grabs a spice jar from the shelf next to him.

"From yourself, mostly."

"From myself?"

"Sure. You were looking a little unhinged after your old man returned to the dust. It was a good time to extract you from the situation."

"Extract me from the situation?" I'm getting shrill now, standing with my fists clenched.

Rust continues to stir the soup, but there's a subtle shift in the way he's standing that tells me he's ready if I decide to go at him. He keeps his voice low and even.

"What are you planning to do? Charge back in there alone?"

"What do you care what I do? You've no right to keep me here!"

"I'm not keeping you anywhere." He sprinkles in a handful of salt and tastes the soup again. "Do you see chains on your wrists? You're free to walk out whenever you like. I just thought you might like some soup first."

His calm quiets me in a way resistance wouldn't have. I'm ready for a fight, but he's not giving me one, and this throws me off balance.

"Soup? You think this is about soup?"

A crooked smile splits his face.

"Everything is about soup. The world looks different when your belly's warm and full. A good bowl of soup can fix just about anything."

"You can keep your soup. Where's my gear? I'm leaving."

His face falls.

"Suit yourself. Your gear is in the next room." He gestures to a low tunnel.

I stomp through the door and find the black stealth armor I stole when we rescued Ianna stacked neatly on a stone shelf. I snap it on, relieved to find it's all there.

Grabbing things is weird. My depth perception is all off with only one eye. But the metal is solid and supportive against my skin, like an old friend who's got your back. I lift the last piece, my warpknife, and snap it into place at my hip. I feel better once I've got it on. I'm glad it's not the standard silver armor. Black seems appropriate.

"Which way out, Jmini?"

"We came in that way." A map flashes up on my retina display, with a blue line showing the path we followed on our way in.

"You tracked our path? Nice work, Jmini."

"Well somebody had to keep their head, and it certainly wasn't going to be you."

I force a chuckle.

"No, I guess it wasn't."

The blue line leads me down a short corridor. It opens up into a medium sized cavern about thirty meters across. As I step out, the Rock Horror looms before me.

I freeze as its massive head snaps in my direction, multi-faceted eyes glowing with an inner radiance. Iridescent green runs along the edge of its torso, fading to black near its tail. Its pincers are nearly two meters long.

I don't know if it's the same Horror that carried me here, but I have to assume it is. Rust can't have more than one pet Rock Horror. Although yesterday I would have said there was no way he could have even that many, so what do I know? Maybe the lunatic breeds them like dogs.

The Rock Horror and I stand perfectly still, watching each other. Like all its kind, the thing is enormous: Its rear thorax is five meters long, and the crown of my head barely comes level with the top of its back. On its upright front body section, the monster's claws flex slowly open and closed. I feel like I'm playing a game of chicken, and the first one to move will be the loser. I carefully stretch my fingers toward my warpknife.

The Horror's multi-faceted eyes sparkle and I feel amusement tinged with disgust, as if the thing finds my movement both funny and offensive. An answering ache pulses in the socket of my bandaged eye.

"You wouldn't think it was so funny if you were in my shoes," I mutter.

The creature cocks its head and flexes its pincers toward me, making my heart stutter. The amusement comes again, coupled with the ache.

"Yeah, you're right. I don't want to fight you. I still don't think it's funny, though." I raise my voice and call back down the tunnel, "Rust! Call off your pet!"

"I thought you didn't need my help." His voice comes from right behind me, making me jump. He's leaning against the doorway, lips quirked up to one side.

"I don't need your help. I just thought you might not want me to kill your dog here.'

He laughs. "I'd like to see you try."

I snatch the warpknife from my belt and crouch into a fighting stance. The Horror goes still, then slowly crouches on six legs, simultaneously raising its pincers.

"Woah, stop. I was joking. Put down your warpknife before someone gets hurt." Rust steps between us, palms outstretched. "That goes for you too." He fixes his gaze on the Horror.

Despite the inhumanity of its face, the creature manages to look embarrassed. It lowers its pincers and takes a few shuffling steps sideways.

I gape at them. "You really talk to it? How is that possible?"

"I use my tongue and my lips, same as everybody else."

"I mean, I know they're supposed to be intelligent, but why would it listen to you?"

"She listens because she chooses to, the same as any person." Rust lays his palm against the creature's carapace. The iridescent green pulses beneath his hand. A thrumming warmth starts up, crossing the cavern in waves.

I cautiously sheath my warpknife. "It's hard to not see a monster when I look at it … I mean her. I've seen Horrors attack Canyon City. I've seen them slice Guardians to shreds."

"Haven't you also seen Outsider bombs explode within the city walls?"

"But those were lies! The IEC planted them to sway public opinion against the Outsiders."

"Are you saying that the IEC controls the narrative? That everything you hear may not be true?"

I scowl at him. "It's not the same thing."

"Fair point." He runs his fingertips down the Horror's carapace like he's petting a cat. The glow follows wherever his hand touches. "But have you ever asked yourself why they're attacking? What their motives might be?"

"They don't need motives. They're killing machines."

"Who told you that?" He turns his gaze toward me, pupils glinting like distant stars.

"The … the IEC," I finish lamely.

"Interesting."

I start to pace. "If the Horrors are so intelligent, why haven't they tried contacting us?"

"What makes you think they haven't?"

"Where are their cities? Where is their technology?"

"Not all intelligent species organize themselves the way we do. Historically speaking, all humans don't either. There are plenty of societies who were nomadic, or whose technology remained undeveloped for one reason or another."

"But colonizing a planet that already has intelligent life would be..."

"Monstrous?"

My mouth works up and down. Even though I kind of knew all this already, it's still a struggle to wrap my mind around just how far the IEC's treachery goes. Everything I've been taught is a lie.

Rust looks at me sympathetically.

"Would you like some soup now?"

I stare at him, my head spinning. I manage a nod. "Yes, I think I would."

2

———

I cup the steaming bowl in my hands, breathing in the salty aroma. The warmth spreads out from my stomach, calming and reassuring. Rust is right. Soup does make everything better. It's a small comforting thing in a world turned upside down.

I stare at Rust over the bowl. The stubble on his chin is silver, the crow's feet at the corners of his eyes are dark creases. Still, his weathered skin doesn't seem that old to me. I'd guess he's somewhere between forty and fifty.

"How did you end up out here?"

He smiles at the question, exposing an incomplete set of teeth.

"How does anyone end up anywhere? The road is simple while you're traveling it. You put one foot in front of the other. It's only when you look back that you realize how far you've come."

"That doesn't answer my question."

He cackles and spoons soup into his mouth.

"I was once like you, believe it or not. Young, efficient, thought I had all the answers."

"I don't think I have all the answers. That's why I'm asking you questions."

"So you can feel as if you have all the answers again. Don't contradict me. I know what it was like to be young and cocky."

"Apparently you know what it's like to be old and difficult too."

He stares at me for a long moment, the flames dancing in his deep-set eyes. Then he shakes his spoon at me. "You are going to test my patience. That's good. I need to be reminded of my own shortcomings. I don't interact with many people out here. It's easy to forget how."

"I think you were getting ready to tell me how you ended up out here," I prompt, trying to steer him back on course.

"Was I? No, I don't think I was."

"What about the Horror then? Do you keep it as a pet? Have you trained it to listen to your commands?"

"Trained it?" He laughs, spraying little specks of soup across the fire. I grimace and wipe one from my cheek. "It's probably more accurate to say that she trained me."

"She?"

He waves this away. "She, he, it. Call her whatever you like. They're asexual most of the time."

"So she trained you? I don't understand."

"She saved my life, I don't know why. I was trapped in a rock fall, alone in a canyon. When I saw her coming, I thought I was dead for sure." He shrugs and examines one hand in the firelight. "I was wrong."

"I don't understand. Does she talk to you?"

"Not in words. But we understand each other well enough."

"Why didn't you tell anyone? This could change everything."

"You think I didn't try?" His mouth twists. "They told me I was crazy. Locked me up and pumped me full of drugs. Nobody wants to hear unpleasant truths."

"But couldn't you show them?"

"Not back then. She was too skittish to come anywhere near Canyon City. Besides, nobody wanted to hear it, least of all the IEC. If I brought her in, we would have both ended up dead. The Hubzoh's intelligence is a closely held secret, and a lot of powerful people are invested in keeping it that way. Heads will roll if it ever comes to light. It'd be a lot easier to make my head roll to keep it in the dark."

"Hubzohs?"

"It's their proper name. You don't think the first scientific expedition named them Horrors do you?"

I slurp the soup while I chew on this information. I can see how "Horror" could easily become slang for "Hubzoh." Then I remember something else.

"What happened while we were assaulting the Mesa? Did the Outsiders survive?"

"Yes. Your advance warning gave them time to evacuate. I don't know if they all made it, but a lot more survived than would have otherwise. You did good."

"Can you take me to them?"

"Sure, if that's what you want to do."

"I don't think I have a choice. I definitely can't go back to Canyon City." I look up as a thought occurs to me. "How long has it been since the attack?"

"About twenty hours. The battle is still going on."

"Why didn't you tell me?" I leap to my feet. "I have to get out there!"

"Do you? Why?"

"Because they're fighting. I should be fighting too."

"Should you? What do you think you could accomplish by yourself?"

I scowl. "What am I supposed to do? Sit here and pretend it's not happening?"

"Do you know the difference between tactics and strategy?"

"I'm not an idiot. I graduated Merrimac, remember?"

Rust continues as if I haven't spoken.

"Tactics are short term solutions to immediate problems. Someone thrusts their warpknife at you, and you parry it. That's a tactic. Strategy is for the big picture. Maneuvering troops to win a battle. Planning a campaign that will win an entire war." He sips his soup and smacks his lips. I fold my arms over my chest.

"Tactically, it might make sense for you to run out there. Maybe you'll kill a few Guardians. Maybe you'll keep them from collapsing a particular Outsider cave system. You might get lucky and see some short-term, tactical gains. But in the big picture? You're not going to change anything."

"So I should ignore the fact that my sister might be dying out there?"

He spreads his hands wide.

"No, you should look past your instinct and examine the big picture. Maybe you lose this battle, but how do you win the war?"

"I'm sure you're going to tell me."

He laughs. "No. I don't have answers. Only questions. How do you defeat an opponent with superior arms and numbers?"

"I don't know, how?"

"I'm asking you."

My scowl gets deeper, but it's not just an expression of annoyance now. I may not like it, but he's got me thinking.

Rust slurps his soup as I hunt for an answer. The silence stretches. Jmini starts playing quiz countdown music in my ear.

"Very funny, Jmini," I subvocalize.

"I'm glad you agree." The AI's voice is deadpan. If he had a face, I'd punch it.

I huff and ignore him, chewing on the question. Rust watches me impassively.

"You need something you can exploit," I finally venture.

"Such as?"

"A weakness."

"Or?"

"Or ... a hidden advantage."

He purses his lips. "Have you got one of those?"

"I don't know," I growl. "I have no idea what resources the Outsiders have. In case you've forgotten, I only came out into the scablands yesterday."

"True. I wasn't necessarily thinking of the Outsiders. Do *you* have one of those?"

"Me? What hidden advantage could I have?"

"I don't know, that's what I'm asking you, isn't it?" His smile is infuriating.

I put my soup bowl down and push myself to my feet.

"You know what? I'm done with your riddles. My sister is out there somewhere. You can talk about strategy and tactics all you want, but I care about people. My dad is dead. Ianna's all I have left. You can help me find her, or you can stay here. Either way, I'm leaving."

3

Rust sighs and puts his bowl down.

"I can see I'm not going to get anything useful out of you until we make sure your sister's all right. I suppose it wasn't a complete waste of time. At least we got a little soup out of it."

He crosses the cavern and pulls a dusty chestplate down from an alcove. Ornamental engraving scrolls around the edges of the armor. The thing is older than I am.

"Are you really going to wear that?"

He cocks an eyebrow at me. "Why wouldn't I?"

"It just … I mean … it's an antique."

He straps the plate to his chest and pulls out a set of greaves.

"So am I. We're meant for each other."

"Yeah, but that armor is ancient. It's got to be twenty years old."

"It's closer to forty." Worn gloves and a dented helmet complete his ensemble.

"But … Why?"

"This armor has saved my life more times than I can count. It's like an old friend. You don't abandon your friends just because they've gotten old."

The last thing he pulls out is a long, curving warpknife. Flourishes of metal wire curl in intricate patterns around the grip. A white greicagin gleams in the center of the pattern.

"That's beautiful," I breathe.

Rust smiles, turning the blade over in his hand. "Yeah, she's a real work of art. Someone special made her for me a long time ago."

Standing in his antique armor, gripping his fancy warpknife, Rust looks like a hero from a story.

"Are you really Captain Steel?"

He stiffens at my words, and his eyes become wistful and sad. Then his expression goes carefully blank, like he's pulling on a mask. He clips the warpknife to his belt.

"That was a long time ago." He strides from the room.

I stare at the place where he stood, my mind whirling. Captain Steel is one of the most famous Guardians of all time. Everyone knows the stories. They say he was the deadliest man with a warpknife who ever lived. He killed a thousand Horrors during the Horror Wars. Every kid who plays at warpknives pretends they're Captain Steel.

Can Rust really be him?

I examine the tiny cave around me. The bottles of spice on the shelves. The old pot cooling beside blackening embers. Such a small, mundane existence. Is this the place legends go to die?

I find him putting a saddle of some kind on his pet Horror, talking to her in a low, reassuring voice. The saddle cinches around the narrow, hinging place where the front part of her body meets her thorax. In front of that, her body is upright, her claws folded at the ready.

Rust climbs up and stands on the saddle, uncoiling a rope with a pair of hooks at the end. He carefully fits the hooks into indentations in the carapace on the sides of the Horror's head: A guidance system of some sort? The monster's carapace pulses green, responding to his gentle words and touch. Rust's back is straight, his movements precise. As if putting on his armor has awakened the old soldier within.

"What happened to you?" I ask.

He doesn't pause in his preparations.

"I told you. Akona saved me. Nobody believed me. Everyone thought I'd lost my mind."

"Akona?"

He smiles and runs his hand over the Horror's back.

"It's not her real name; they don't use words like we do. But it's what I call her. It feels right."

I say the name again, examining the round shape in my mouth. The Horror pulses in response, trails of light rippling along her carapace. He's right. It does feel right.

Akona carries us with the surety of a clifftoe. Her six legs work together, keeping her back so level it's almost like riding a gravbike. If gravbikes were the size of transport trucks, that is. Even the narrow part of Akona's body is almost too wide for a human to sit comfortably, making my legs stretch across the saddle. It's so dark in the tunnels, I can't even see my nose on my face.

"It's like being a deep diver all over again," I mutter.

Rust sits on the saddle in front of me, the guiding rope held loosely in his hands. He's clearly letting Akona navigate. A faint red outline surrounds him, like the ghost of my greicagin-sight. I concentrate on it and his image becomes clearer. Around him, a light painting of the cavern comes into focus as well.

"Is that what you did before?" he asks. "You were a deep diver?"

"Yeah, I was part of Papa Grady's operation. Before I qualified for the Guardian Tournament."

"Did you like it?"

I snort. "I was never given a choice. But I suppose I liked being down in the deep dark. Squeezing into crevices no other human has ever set foot in. I was good at it too. I had a knack for finding greicagin deposits. It was like I could smell them."

"Do you mean feel them?"

The question makes me sit up.

"Yeah, that's exactly what I mean. How did you know?"

"I feel them too."

"You do?" I lean away from him in the saddle. I've never met anyone who feels greicagins the way I do; it makes me suspicious.

Maybe Rust is telling me what he thinks I want to hear. "What do they feel like?"

"They itch. Make my skin tingle."

Well, if he's making it up, he's doing a good job of it.

"That's what they do to me too," I admit.

"I thought they might."

"Why would you think that?"

"Well, you can hear Akona, can't you? That's a pretty strong clue."

I shake my head, not following. "What does Akona have to do with greicagins?"

He turns in the saddle in front of me. His metal-sheen eyes glow like greicagin shards in the dark.

"You haven't figured it out yet? Greicagins are Hubzoh eggs."

I sway as the realization hits me. Of course. That's why we found greicagins in places that had been mined out. That's why we kept running into Horrors in those places.

"We use their eggs as fuel?" My horrified gaze turns to the green greicagin shard gleaming in the handle of my warpknife. "We put them in our warpknives? No wonder they try to kill us."

"Well, yes and no. They don't think of eggs the same way we do."

"What do you mean?"

"As far as I can tell, ninety percent of their eggs never hatch. I don't know why that is, you'd have to ask a scientist. What I do know is that once the Hubzoh have laid them, they forget about them. The eggs are on their own."

"So… they don't mind us harvesting their eggs?"

"'Don't mind' might be putting it a bit too strongly. They mind. They just don't mind in the same way you or I would mind if someone were harvesting our family. Their issue is that we harvest the eggs before the ten percent have had a chance to hatch."

"Our mines are committing xenocide."

"Essentially, yes. We're harvesting their future generations before they ever have a chance."

I become acutely aware of Akona beneath me. Is she listening? Can she understand what we're saying?

I shift uncomfortably in the saddle.

"How long have you two been together?"

"Longer than you've been alive."

"Does she have children?"

"Probably."

"What do you mean probably? If you've been together over eighteen years, wouldn't you know if she had children?"

"I told you, they don't raise their children the way we do. Hubzoh young are self-sufficient from the moment they hatch. Whether they survive or not has nothing to do with their parents."

"So, Akona wouldn't even know if she had children?"

"Not as far as I know."

I shake my head, mystified.

"I guess that shows why they don't care very much about the greicagins. If they never even see their children, why would they care if they hatch or not?"

"I told you, they do care." Rust's voice sharpens to a hard edge. "They just don't care in the same way humans would care."

"OK, you don't have to get snippy about it. I get it."

But I don't get it, not really. If you care about someone, you look out for them. That's what take care means, isn't it? That you take care of them?

To me, the Hubzoh method of leaving their young to fend for themselves is a pretty clear indication of how they really feel about their children.

4

It's still raining when we reach the surface. The clouds weep steady tears over the scablands. Muddy streams gouge the desert floor, cutting deep channels into the sand and clay. There's no sign of the Guardian assault. No sign of anything at all beyond the steady grey downpour and the slow slump of sandstone turning to mud.

"Now what?" I squint and wipe water out of my good eye.

Rust pulls his brown hood over his head. "Now we start looking."

"Why did we come to the surface? Wouldn't it be safer to stay underground?"

"Normally, yes. But not during monsoon season. The rain makes everything fall in. We're likely to get buried by a mudslide if we stay underground."

I nod. He's right: The monsoons transform the Five Canyons every year, dissolving walls that have stood for centuries while building others in their place.

A few years ago, a chasm divided Papa Grady's camp overnight. I woke to find my little tent perched on the lip of a ravine thirty meters deep. If I'd been camped half a meter to the side, it would have swallowed me in my sleep.

It took three weeks to build a rickety bridge reconnecting the two sides of the divided camp. I was lucky, I happened to be on the same side as the mess hall. Those on the other side had to survive on whatever food we could throw across to them. They were a skinny bunch by the time we finally got the bridge built.

I pull up my tattered hood, grateful for the worn cloak Rust has loaned me.

"How will we find them?" I ask.

"Don't worry. I've got a few tricks up my sleeve."

Akona pads forward, her feet sinking into the soft ground with every step. Her narrow feet stab in and out of the mud like sharpened stakes. She moves in little bursts, covering a hundred meters in a frantic dash, then freezing beside a spire or cliff face. During these pauses, only her multi-faceted eyes move, shining with oily iridescence.

"Jmini, can you tell me where we are?" I whisper.

"Not with any great degree of accuracy. The clouds prevent me from using the sun or stars to triangulate our position, and we're all out of drones. There are a lot of ambient signals bouncing around approximately five kilometers to the southwest. I would guess that is Canyon City. However, it is only a guess."

I tap on Rust's shoulder and point. "Is Canyon City that way?"

"Yeah. How'd you know?" He turns to look at me.

I smile. "I've got a few tricks up my sleeve."

He eyes me for a moment, then grunts and faces forward again.

"You can keep your secrets if it makes you feel better."

"Says the mysterious hermit who skulks around the scablands in a ragged cloak."

"I'm old. I've earned the right to be eccentric."

I'm thinking up a smart retort when Akona veers sharply, nearly throwing me from the saddle. I flail and clutch a handful of Rust's cloak to keep from falling.

"What the dust?"

"Trouble." Jmini registers it a split second before I do.

A trio of gravbikes come speeding into view half a kilometer up the canyon. They bank around a cliff face at high speed, spraying up rooster tails forty meters long. They complete the turn and stabilize on their new course. Headed straight for us.

"Spines." I cast my eyes around for cover, but they've caught us right in the middle of one of Akona's dashes. We're trapped in the open, with nowhere to hide. "Why aren't we running?"

"No point. They've already seen us." Rust swings his legs to one side and slides to the ground.

"What do we do?"

"We're riding a Rock Horror, Twist. What kind of conclusions do you think they'll draw from that?"

"I don't know." Even as the words leave my lips, I know they're a lie. I've got a pretty good idea what a can of Guardians is going to think of someone who rides a Rock Horror. It isn't good.

I slide to the ground beside Rust and push my hood back. I try to ignore the flutter in my stomach as the gravbikes brake to a halt ten meters away.

At least they didn't just open fire. That's something.

The Guardians dismount, their silver boots sinking into the mud. There's two short men and a tall, lean woman. Thankfully, I don't recognize any of them. They draw their warpknives, eyes moving uncertainly from Akona to us and back again. Finally, the woman steps forward.

"Who are you? What are you doing out here?" The fringe of her blonde hair peeks out beneath her helmet. Her blue eyes are cold.

"We're just traveling through." Rust keeps his voice calm, his hands away from his warpknife. "We're not looking for any trouble."

"Step away from the Horror. We'll protect you."

"I'm afraid I can't do that. She's a friend of mine." Rust's smile doesn't reach his voice.

"Horrors don't have friends." One of the men speaks up. He's got a square jaw and dark stubble shading his chin. He points his warpknife at Rust. "What kind of man is friends with a Horror?"

"If you'd stop stabbing them the moment you see them, more of them might try to be friendly."

"They're murdering fiends." The third man's voice rumbles like a rockslide. He's built like a boulder too: as wide as he is tall, and all muscle.

"Well, from their point of view, humans are the murdering fiends." Rust keeps his tone reasonable, but his words draw angry glares from the Guardians.

I slide my hand toward my warpknife. I have a feeling this isn't going to end well.

"Everybody just stay calm. Nobody has to get hurt here." Tension makes my voice squeak a little at the end. I guess I'm not as good at pretending to be calm as Rust.

"Shut up, deserter," the woman snaps. "We'll deal with you after we take care of the Horror."

Shock jolts the length of my spine. Did they recognize me?

"Deserter?" I sputter. "What do you…?"

"Cut the act. You're out here in the middle of nowhere with a Horror and a madman. What you are is obvious." Contempt drips from the woman's words.

"Why don't you tell us how you really feel?" Jmini murmurs.

"This is your last chance," she continues. "Drop your weapons and step away from the Horror."

I look at Rust. He shrugs and sighs.

"I'm afraid we can't do that."

The boulder man steps forward.

"What makes you think you have a choice?"

Rust's warpknife blooms in his grip. I hesitate a heartbeat, then draw mine as well. The thin woman is right. I am a deserter. I've already fought against the Guardians once. There's no turning back now.

5

Our warpknives blaze twin arcs, rain sizzling along their edges as we face down the Guardians.

The woman's mouth opens in surprise. The square-jawed man's face stays hard and businesslike: He's just doing his job.

But it's the third member of the can that comes for me. The Boulder's eyes shine with sadistic joy behind the red curve of his warpknife. He's the type that enjoys violence. He'll hurt me just because he can.

I sink into a guard position and circle to my right, keeping my good eye facing my antagonist. I take small steps, wary of my footing in the slippery mud.

The Boulder smiles as he closes on me. He looks eager. Like he can't wait to carve my face from my skull.

In my peripheral vision I see the other man approaching Akona, while the woman closes on Rust. At least we've got even numbers. Maybe we've got a chance.

Then the man is on me, and I don't have any more time to think.

He feints a slash, testing my reflexes. I step back, but my back foot slides in the mud, dropping me to one knee.

He seizes his chance, lunging in to skewer me. I parry and roll, and come up dripping mud. The slice across my forearm shows me how bad my parry was. Having only one eye is throwing off my depth perception.

The Boulder bares his teeth in an evil grin. He already knows he's got me. He's going to take his time and savor the kill.

Behind him I see the lean woman pressing Rust. She's fast, flicking a rapid series of probing cuts at him, one after another. Rust hardly moves, parrying each thrust with tiny shifts of his blade. He barely looks like he's fighting. Maybe all those stories about Captain Steel weren't exaggerations.

Akona screams, and the sound pierces my skull like a rock-hammer. Hot pain blooms in my injured eye, exploding out through my skull.

Something happens inside my mind, and the world shifts.

Gone is the mud and rain and grey, replaced by lines of red power. My greicagin sight. My warpknife blazes in my grip, and the other warpknives shine like a miniature constellation around me.

But it's Akona that draws my attention.

She's shining like a sun among us, light exploding out of her, ten times as bright as any of our blades. I stare at her in awe.

Rust was right. The greicagins do come from the Horrors. Akona is a brilliant star, overflowing with power.

I'm so mesmerized, I almost get skewered on the spot.

The sizzling arc of the Boulder's blade comes slicing down at my face, carving a trail of light.

"Twist!" Jmini screams.

My instincts and boosted reflexes throw me to one side, before my stunned brain has time to process. I'm thankful for all the hours of training Instructor Skinn made us do. The hours of falling and diving and rolling, over and over. At the time I thought they were monotonous and boring. Now I'm pretty sure they just saved my life.

I roll across the mud, trying to get my bearings. The real world is back, all mud and rain and grey, but the greicagin energy world is still there too. Buzzing around me like a ghost. Like a virtual display laid on top of reality.

I can see the Boulder with my mind, his bright warpknife coming after me as I roll.

I sweep a kick at his legs. It doesn't bring him down, but it forces him to step back, which gives me time to scramble back onto my feet.

I crouch to parry his next blow, but the competing versions of reality blur together. My good eye sees only mud and rain, while my bandaged one shows me a world of blurring power. I shake my head, trying to bring them together, trying to figure out what's real.

The warpknife plunging toward my chest is real.

I try to parry, but do I parry the metal blade or the blazing arc of power? They don't quite line up in my sight, the power pushing out ahead of the metal.

I miss badly, and fire pierces my guts.

The pain is like nothing I've ever felt before. Like being skewered by a welding torch. My entire universe shrinks to that small, bright ball of pain inside me.

The warpknife falls from my hand as I gurgle and tumble to the mud.

This is it. This is the end. I lie curled around the fire in my guts, waiting for the final blow. The stroke that finishes me.

But the only thing that comes down is the rain, cold and soothing on my feverish skin.

I'm dimly aware of movement around me. Of cries and grunts of pain. Of bodies fighting and falling.

Then there is silence and stillness; it seems to go on for a long time.

The pain flares as gloved hands roll me over, scooping me up out of the mud. Broken things grate sickeningly within me. I try to scream, but all that comes out is a moan.

"Easy, boy. I've got you." Rust's arms are strong beneath me. His cloak smells like soup and smoke.

I'm dimly aware of a red sun approaching, then a gentle, lulling motion. After that, there's nothing at all.

6

The scent of smoke drifts into the red world of my dream. I'm deep underground, and the glowing greicagin-dust walls branch out like arteries around me. Sound comes next. The clink of equipment. The hum of many voices.

I surface slowly, unsure where my dream ends and reality begins. I'm lying on a cot, beneath a dusty green blanket. Bandages wrap my midsection. Soft-glow lamps light the room. I'm alone, but I can hear other people moving around outside the door.

Where am I? This isn't Rust's cave, that's for sure.

I blink my good eye, trying to focus. The red of my greicagin sight still lies over the stone around me, but it's fading into the background as my mind wakes.

"Jmini? Do you know where we are?"

"Yes, I do."

"Would you like to share that information?"

"If you insist." Jmini sounds peevish.

I can't imagine what's gotten him upset, but I have more important things to worry about right now. Like where the dust I am and how I got here.

It looks like I'm in a medical unit. My cot is one of several lined up along the wall. All but one are filled with bandaged forms. The woman next to me is missing an arm. The man beside her has casts on both his legs.

I probe the bandages around my stomach with my fingers. It's sore, but nothing like the all-devouring pain that was there before. Wherever I am, they've done a good job patching me up.

"We're in a hidden Outsider complex," Jmini supplies.

"That's what I figured. How long have we been here?"

"Four days."

"Four days?" I whistle through my teeth. I must have been hurt bad. Four days is a long time to be unconscious.

"Do you always talk to yourself out loud?" The woman in the next cot is staring at me, her eyes dark and serious above prominent cheekbones. She's got a wide nose and her black hair has been shaved down to stubble. Her left arm ends in a ball of bandages just below her shoulder.

"Sorry. I didn't realize anyone else was awake."

"I wasn't. You woke me up." The words could be accusing, but they're not. Just a simple statement of fact.

"Again, I'm sorry. I'll keep my voice down next time."

She examines me with suspicious eyes.

"You're not one of us. What are you doing here?"

"That's a good question. Me, myself, and I were just trying to figure that out."

"You're a Guardian." She spits the word.

"Reformed, actually. I've been working inside the wall, stealing information for the resistance."

Her mouth makes a surprised circle. "That sounds dangerous."

"No more than being out here with you." I nod toward her severed arm.

"I suppose not." She blushes and gives me a tight smile. "I'm Ghena. Sorry about the suspicion."

"Twist. Don't worry about it. If those bastards had blown off my arm, I'd be suspicious too. Where are we anyway? I was unconscious when they brought me in."

A new voice comes from the doorway. "You're alive. That's really all you need to worry about right now."

The creases in the woman's face are deeper than the last time I saw her. Her dreadlocks are heavy with crimson dust. Still, despite the tiredness, she looks as solid as a granite spire.

"Tempest. It's good to see you."

"I wish I could say the same. Can you walk, or should I get a wheelchair?"

"Uh, I don't know. I haven't tried to stand yet."

"Well, get on with it. I don't have all day."

Ghena is watching us with wide eyes, clearly awed by Tempest's presence. I give her a smile and a shrug.

"I guess I've got to go. It was nice meeting you. Heal up fast."

She squeaks out, "You too."

"Come on, Twist. There's a war happening," Tempest barks.

I roll my eyes at Ghena and swing my legs over the side of the cot. The stone is smooth and cold against the bottom of my feet. I lean forward and push myself up. My stomach tenses as I push, and a shock of pain crackles through me. I sway, grabbing onto the wall for support, then stand there taking sharp, shallow breaths, waiting for the pain to ebb.

"Wheelchair it is." Tempest grabs my elbow and steers me toward the chair. I want to resist, but each step tears at my insides, shooting pain up and down my body. Two steps are enough to convince me I'm not strong enough to walk.

"You should really get some medrigs out here." I grit my teeth as Tempest lowers me into the wheelchair. "Save us all a lot of pain."

"What a great suggestion. I don't know why I never thought of that." Tempest pushes the wheelchair forward violently. She does not sound amused.

"Just a thought."

"Your thoughts got some of my best people killed. I suggest you keep your thoughts to yourself."

Fair point.

Filthy, exhausted people lie propped against the walls of the tunnel. We thread a narrow path among them, avoiding outstretched legs. The floor beneath my wheelchair is level and polished: This complex has been here a long time.

"How did this place escape the bombing?"

"It's one of our fallbacks. It hasn't been used in years."

I examine the tired, dirty faces of the refugees as Tempest wheels me past. I don't see the fear and despair I expect; instead I find anger and determination. These people are down, but they're not done fighting. Not by a long shot.

The first face I see in the council room is Rust. The second is Ianna.

"You're alive!" I smile, reaching out my hands to my sister. Seeing her so big is still a shock: In my mind she's a kid, not this lanky teenager.

She doesn't reach back. Her mouth is a hard, angry line.

"No thanks to you."

I feel like she's punched me in the stomach.

"What?"

"You killed Dad," she chokes. "I got him back for one whole night and you killed him again."

"But … you wanted me to kill Julius."

"Julius! Not Dad!" Tears stream down her cheeks. My eyes fill in response.

"I'm sorry. I did my best."

"Your best wasn't very good, Theo. Your best was a spine-choked dust heap."

Tears are rolling down my cheeks now too. I don't wipe them away.

"You're right. The attack was a disaster. Mai died. Dad died. Shadow and Knott could be dead. I'd be dead too if it wasn't for Rust." I hold her gaze, our faces awash in tears. "I'm sorry. If I could take it all back, I would. But I can't. All I can do is keep fighting, and try to honor their memory."

"That's all any of us can do." Tempest steps between us, breaking our death stare. "Let's put the family drama aside. You can blame each other all you want when this war is over. We don't have time for this right now."

Ianna folds her arms over her chest and turns away. I swallow a lump, and wipe the back of my hand across my eyes. There will be time for tears later.

7

———

Tempest parks my chair next to Rust. There are a dozen people around a large table I don't recognize. Hard-faced men and women bristling with weapons. The man directly across from me has a ridge of Outsider scabs running from his left eyebrow back above his ear. He catches me looking and stares at me until I avert my gaze.

Tempest takes her place at the head of the table and clicks a display to life in front of her. "This is being broadcast live all over Canyon City right now."

In the display, Julius stands atop the wall, the wind whipping his ash-blond hair. His cheeks are red from the cold. Behind him, five rusty cages hang from thick chains. Five prisoners sit shackled on the ground. Their tattoos and scabs mark them as Outsiders. I don't recognize any of them, but the hiss of breath around the room tells me I'm in the minority.

"Traitors! Rebels! Terrorists!" Julius rages, stabbing at the prisoners with his finger. The Outsiders tremble, the whites of their eyes showing.

A pair of Guardians grab the first Outsider, a woman whose blonde hair is matted with dark blood. They drag her into one of the cages and stretch out her arms. She struggles, but they hold her as easily as if they were carved from stone.

A third Guardian approaches, towering over the others, brandishing a silver hammer. A growl forms deep in my throat. Ghengis. That psychopath looks right at home.

The woman screams while Ghengis hammers long spikes through her outstretched hands, nailing her to the sides of the cage. Then he does the same to her feet.

Someone crumples to the floor in our little meeting chamber, wailing and weeping. I don't see who it is. I can't tear my eyes away from the display.

My stomach churns and bucks as Ghengis nails the other four Outsiders into their cages. Then the cages are lowered over the side of the wall on massive chains. The Outsiders will hang there, flayed by the wind and sand, until there is nothing left in the cages but bone.

Julius comes back into the frame, looking directly into the camera. "This is what happens to the enemies of Canyon City. Turn in your neighbors before it's too late. Anyone caught withholding information or helping the Outsiders in any way will end up in a cage just like this."

The camera pans back to the hanging cages and the five impaled figures inside. Fresh blood streaks the rusty metal. The feed goes dark.

Seething rage burns through me, my hands clenched in shaking fists. The atrocities all trace back to one man. Julius enslaved my sister. Julius cut out my eye. Julius killed my dad.

"That man's an animal." The collapsed woman sobs from the floor. "Fiona…"

"I'm sorry for your loss, Vi. Your sister deserves better than that." Tempest says. She takes a shaky breath and raises her head, her eyes catching each of us in turn. "In case anyone needed a reminder, this is what we're up against. We can't reason with them. There will be no negotiation, no deals. We win this fight or we die, it's that simple."

I nod solemnly, my jaw clenched. Julius Carlyle will pay for what he's done.

A topographical map of the scablands flickers to life in front of her.

Red icons indicate Guardian troop placements. The Outsider complexes are in blue.

"This is where things stand as far as I know. Talk to me. What do you all know that I don't. Deet?" She looks at a short, light-skinned man with broad shoulders.

He nods and steps forward, pointing out various icons as he speaks. "The eastern front is collapsing. All the complexes in this valley are gone." He gestures, and three blue icons turn black. "I don't expect these" —he lights up another four— "to last more than a couple days."

Tempest frowns. "Evacuate all non-fighting personnel. Send them to Broken Rock." She lights up a complex icon several kilometers away.

"Broken Rock is already near capacity," a young woman says apologetically. She's got a long, thin face, and blue tattoos on her skull beneath a fine layer of stubble. She can't be older than sixteen.

"How many more can you take, Lane?" Tempest doesn't miss a beat.

The girl hesitates, wringing her hands.

"No more than a thousand. Five hundred would be better."

"A thousand it is. You and Deet work out the details between you." Tempest never takes her eyes off the map. "What about the Molten Valley? Maddi?"

It goes on like that for a while. Each of the Outsiders steps forward to update what's been happening in their sector of the map. The news is not good. By the time they've all given their reports, almost twenty of the blue Outsider icons have turned black, and almost none of the Guardian icons have. Silence falls after the last Outsider finishes speaking. We stare glumly at the map, taking in our impending doom.

"What about allies?" I venture. "There are four other colonies out there. Is there anyone in the Five Canyons we can ask for help? What about White Rock? Or Twin Spires?"

Tempest laughs bitterly. "Of course, why didn't we think of that before?"

"There's no need for sarcasm, Tempest," Deet chides her softly. "The kid might have a point."

She shoots him a hard look but waves her hand for him to continue.

He takes a deep breath, then releases his words all in a rush. "I know you don't want to think about it, but maybe it's time to reach out to the Forsaken."

Everyone tries to speak at once. Voices are raised, and in seconds people are shouting to be heard. I shrink back in my wheelchair. I don't know who these Forsaken are, but they're obviously a polarizing subject.

Tempest lets the debate rage for a minute, then raises her hands for silence. Everyone ignores her. She shouts, but her voice just becomes part of the din. Finally, she slams her cane across the table. The map blips out, plunging the room into darkness. The Outsiders are startled into silence.

"Thank you." A single light shines up from the table, putting a spotlight on her face. "Obviously, we all have strong opinions on the Forsaken. Deet, since you brought them up, I'll let you go first. What in the dust-choked netherworld makes you think we can trust the Forsaken?"

The light shifts position, spotlighting Deet now. He swallows nervously.

"I don't know if we can trust them. But I do know they hate the Guardians as much as we do. And we're running out of options."

"The enemy of my enemy is my friend? I don't know if that applies to the Forsaken." Lane's voice is slow and serious.

"I'm sorry, but who are the Forsaken?" I ask.

"The Forsaken are a bunch of outlaws living deep in the wastes," Rust explains.

"How does that make them different from the Outsiders?"

"The Outsiders are a community," Tempest says. "We're trying to make a better society out here. One that's about improving people's lives, not increasing the IEC's bottom line. The Forsaken are different."

"They're animals," Lane says. "They prey upon everyone: Merchant caravans, IEC trains, Outsider settlers, it doesn't matter to them. Anyone not Forsaken is an enemy as far as they're concerned."

"Why haven't I heard of them before?" I ask.

"There aren't any Forsaken camps near Canyon City. They stay far out in the scablands."

"Not all of them," Rust corrects. "There's a large group near Sapphire City."

"Which is almost a thousand kilometers away," Lane says.

Rust nods. "True."

"So why would they help us? It doesn't sound like they have anything to do with Canyon City," I ask.

"Enemy of my enemy," Deet says. "They hate the IEC as much as we do."

"But they hate us too," Lane repeats.

"Yes, but I'd argue they hate us less than they hate the IEC." Deet leans forward, his hands braced on the table. "Maybe we could convince them to fight on our side."

"And how would we do that?" Tempest's expression is skeptical.

"We offer them something they don't have," Rust says.

"And what's that?"

"I don't know. I'd have to ask them to find out."

Tempest stares at the map, her eyebrows drawn low. For a long minute, the only movement comes from her lavender irises flicking over the battle lines. Finally, she sighs.

"I don't see what we have to lose by sending an emissary. It's probably a suicide mission, though."

"I'll go," Deet says. "It was my idea."

"No. I need you here. You've got too many people depending on you."

"Let me go." The words are out of my mouth before I can stop them. Heat rises to my cheeks as everyone looks at me. "I'm not needed here. And I'd like a chance to make up for my disastrous attack on the Mesa.

"I'll go too," Rust says. "Someone needs to babysit the pup. He's not going to be in any shape to fight for a while. And I think we have a lot to talk about."

I catch his metallic eyes and nod.

"Sounds like we got here just in time." My heart lifts at the familiar voice.

Shadow stands in the doorway. Her dark eyes flash, taking in the room at a glance, gathering information the way she's been trained. She's a tiny silhouette in her thin, black Covert armor, helmet tucked under her arm, kinky hair sticking out in her trademark twists. Knott looms behind Shadow, fringe of shaggy black hair hanging straight down over her forehead, twice as big as the little Covert in her bulky Tank armor. Knott's broad, honest face splits in a toothy smile.

Relief floods through me, summoning an answering grin. My friends made it out. My crew is alive. Despite my dad being dead and my sister being mad at me and Julius Carlyle being governor and the Outsiders being on the edge of extermination, for a single shining moment, all is right with the world. With Shadow and Knott by my side, anything is possible.

Shadow winks at me. "You didn't think you were going to get rid of us that easily, did you?"

8

"Are you sure this is going to work?"

I'm lying back on my cot, with Rust standing over me. Shadow and Knott are off gathering gear for our mission.

He shrugs. "No. But it's worth a shot. The greicagins in your bloodstream are helping your body heal already. Maybe I can speed the process along."

I'm dubious, but I keep my mouth shut. What do I have to lose? If he fails, nothing happens, and I have a very painful journey ahead of me. If he succeeds, maybe it's a bit less painful.

"What do you think, Jmini?" I subvocalize carefully. "Will this help?"

"You're asking an AI about magic? That's hardly my area of expertise."

"Oh, come on. My implants are already speeding up the healing process, and they're powered by my greicagin chip. Can that process be boosted or not?"

"When you put it like that, it almost sounds like science. So in a scientific sense, yes, the healing factors in your implants can be boosted if you give them more power. Grab did something similar with that dataspike when you were locked up in the Mesa."

"Doesn't sound like magic to me."

"No, the magic part comes when some scabland vagrant does the boosting with the power of his mind."

Rust lays his hands on my chest. I can feel the thick calluses on his fingertips. He looks me in the eye.

"Ready?"

I nod. Whether it's magic or science, I'm in favor of anything that will get me back on my feet faster.

Rust closes his eyes, and for a moment nothing happens. Then his hands begin to glow.

It takes me a second to realize I'm not seeing anything with my good eye. To it, his hands look perfectly normal. But to my blind eye, my greicagin-sight, his hands get brighter by the second, shining like flitbats.

I watch the light move from his hands into my chest. It seeps down through my skin, like water through rock, but it doesn't feel like water. It feels like heat. Like the desert sun on my skin.

The shard beneath my collarbone grows warm in response, and the heat spreads through my body, pooling around the wound in my stomach. It gathers there, slowly intensifying until it burns, making me gasp.

"Are you all right?" Rust's forehead wrinkles with concern.

"Fine." I grunt. "I think it's working. Keep going."

He watches my face for a moment, then nods, turning his attention back to my wound. The flow of light and heat intensifies.

Spines. It burns like a small star being born in my belly.

I grit my teeth, tears leaking from the corners of my eyes. I'm being cooked from the inside.

"Enough!" I push his hands away from my chest and curl onto my side, whimpering. My breath rattles, ragged in my throat.

Rust takes a step back. "Did I hurt you?"

"Give me a minute."

I lie there like a flat rock after sunset, the heat slowly leeching away. After a few minutes, the burn is nothing more than a low warmth. I'm no longer being broiled alive; now it's merely a slow-cook.

"That was intense." I release a long, shuddering breath.

Rust eyes me cautiously. "Did it work?"

"I don't know. It did something, that's for sure. Felt like I was being roasted on a spit." I roll over and carefully lever myself up until I'm sitting on the edge of the cot. I grin. "That hurt a lot less than it did on the way down."

Rust returns my smile.

"I'm glad. I guess I've learned a thing or two after all."

"How did you do that? I could see you pushing energy into my chest. Your hands were glowing like stars."

"You could see that?"

I explain to him about my greicagin-sight, and how it's gotten stronger in my blind eye. "It's always there now. Like a ghost image laid on top of reality."

Rust's eyes grow serious.

"That's impressive. I knew you were in tune with the Horrors and the gins, but to see them all the time? I can't even do that."

"How did you know?"

He grins at me.

"How do you think you hear Akona? I told you. The Hubzoh, the greicagins, they're all connected."

"Can everyone feel it?"

"No, just a few."

"Why?"

"I don't know. I used to think it had something to do with our exposure to greicagins, or the concentration of greicagin particles in our bloodstream. But that doesn't really hold sand. As you know, greicagin particles are in the stone, the sand, the dust: Everywhere. Every person in Canyon City breathes them in on a daily basis. Yet most people show no signs of sensitivity."

"But there have been other people like us?"

"I've known a few, yes."

"Where are they now?"

His face closes.

"That's a story for another time. Come on, the others are waiting for us."

9

As we move through the tunnels, I marvel at how much better I feel. My stomach still hurts, but the pain is only a deep ache. Like I was punched in the stomach by Ghengis, not run through with a warpknife. Whatever Rust did with those greicagins is almost as good as spending the night in a medrig.

We meet Shadow and Knott inside a large cavern that's being used as a vehicle depot. They're loading gear into a massive truck with an open bed.

I eye the thing skeptically. "We're taking that beast?"

Shadow shrugs.

"It's not my first choice either. But vehicles are at a premium. We're lucky they're not making us walk." She lays her hand on the massive side panel. "I dub thee Beast. May you carry us far and fast."

I grunt and circle the Beast. It's got a double-bench cab in the front, and twin cannons on a swivel mount in the open bed.

"My seat." Knott pats the cannon mount and grins at me.

"You're welcome to it. It'll be as hot as the surface of the sun out there with no shade."

Knott frowns.

"I did not think about that."

"We'll pack you a big floppy sun hat." Shadow grins. "Maybe pin a few reaper blossoms to the brim."

Knott does not look amused.

Someone clears their throat behind me. I turn to find my sister staring at the floor.

"Have you got a minute?" She fidgets with the sleeve of her loose shirt.

I hesitate. "I've got gear to pack, but … sure, I've got a minute."

"I wanted to say I'm sorry for snapping at you earlier. I know you didn't kill Dad on purpose."

"I didn't kill Dad at all! Julius killed him," I yelp, instantly defensive.

"That's what I meant. Let me finish!"

"Sorry." I force myself to take a breath. "I'm as upset about it as you are. He was my dad too, you know."

"I know, and now he's dead and I didn't even get a chance to say goodbye. I barely got a chance to say hello."

"It wasn't…"

"Shut it, Theo!"

"My name is Twist."

She growls. "Twist. Theo. Whatever your name is. I'm trying to say you're all the family I have left. Be careful. Don't die out there, ok?"

"Fine. I won't."

She finally catches my eye as I huff my reply. She's got the same look in her eye as when we were kids and we realized we were doing something dumb, and Dad was probably going to punish us for it. A startled laugh bursts from my lips. After a second, she laughs too.

"I'm still mad at you." She punches me in the chest. "But I don't want anything to happen to you either. I'm the only one that gets to hurt you, OK?"

"OK." I want to hug her, but I don't think she'd like that. So I hold out my hand to shake instead. "Friends?"

She eyes my hand like it's a sand stinger, then reaches out and taps it with her fingers. It's not a shake, but maybe it's as close as she can get right now. She looks up into my eyes.

"Not friends. Family."

I nod and repeat the word.

"Family."

"And I'm coming with you."

"What?"

"I said I'm coming with you." She hefts a small gear bag I hadn't noticed.

"No. Absolutely not. It's too dangerous."

"So you want me to stay here and worry while you go out and risk your life?"

"No, but…"

"Then I'm coming." She sets her jaw the same way she always has when she's being stubborn. I see the echoes of hundreds of past arguments in her eyes.

"Ianna, be reasonable. I'm trained for this. I've got armor. There's no sense in both of us being killed."

"So you admit you're going out to be killed now?"

"No, that's not…"

"I'm going with you, Theo. End of story. You can't stop me."

We stare at each other, locked in a silent battle of wills.

Ianna has been changed by our years apart. She was always stubborn, but there's steel behind her eyes now. She's been weathered by the storm.

There's something dangerous in them too. Something that makes my fingers want to stray toward the handle of my warpknife.

Thunder rumbles in the distance and the cavern trembles beneath my boots. Dust drifts down from the ceiling. An alarm shrills.

Tempest charges into the hangar, her boots ringing on the stone.

"Nice to see you kids are getting reacquainted, but it's time to go. We're under attack." Firm and in charge, she plants her feet wide.

"Tell Ianna she can't come with us, Tempest. It's too dangerous." I know I sound like a five year old, but I can't help it.

Tempest's mouth puckers like she's tasting something sour.

"I'm not your mother. Not her mother either. Girl can make her own decisions."

"But it's not safe!"

"You think it's safe here? Did you see Julius nail those people into cages? Do you hear the bombs? This is war, Twist. There's nowhere on this planet that's safe right now. Your sister is probably safer with you than anywhere. At least she'll have her brother looking out for her."

"But…" My protest dies in my mouth. She's right. As long as Julius is in charge, no place is truly safe. And I should protect Ianna myself. Isn't that the whole reason I became a Guardian? To protect my sister?

I turn back to Ianna. Her eyes are still challenging, but I see wary hope in them too.

"Fine. You can come. But you have promise to follow orders. We'll need to work as a team out there, and one wrong step could endanger us all. Can you do that?"

Ianna nods. "I'm on your side, Theo … Twist. I just want to help."

"Fine, load up. Shadow, make sure she's geared up properly, OK?"

Tempest walks us to the hangar door. Pale dust speckles her dreadlocks, and the explosions are a rolling, distant drumbeat.

"Aren't you worried about the attack?" I ask.

"This happens all the time. They're bombing the surface, but they don't really know where we are. We're too deep for them to do any real damage with surface bombs."

"What if they figure out where you are?"

"Then we fight." Her face is calm, her eyes hard. This is a woman prepared to die for her freedom. She gestures at the Beast, and my crew. "And you don't need to worry. They're bombing the next valley over. The exit to the hangar should be clear. Do you have everything you need?"

Rust waggles his hand at her. "Everything covers a lot of ground. But we've got a good crew, and we're as prepared as can be expected. If anyone can get across a thousand kilometers of scabland in the middle of a war, it's us."

Tempest looks us over, catching and holding each of our gazes in turn.

"Thank you for your bravery. Our hopes and dreams of a better world go with you. It's a long shot, but your mission could save thousands of lives and tip the balance toward freedom from IEC tyranny. May the sun be at your back."

Akona waits for Rust outside the cavern. The old hermit swings easily into the saddle. I eye the Hubzoh skeptically.

"Is she going to be able to keep up with the Beast?"

Rust cocks an eyebrow and smirks at me.

"The question is, will the Beast be able to keep up with her?"

10
———

"I still can't believe he's riding a Horror."

Shadow stares out the window of the truck, her expression somewhere between terror, disgust, and awe. Off to our left, Akona shines faintly in the darkness, green and yellow rippling down her back.

"Their real name is Hubzoh," I correct her. " 'Horror' is a derogatory term."

"Obviously it's derogatory. I don't think anyone would be called Horror as a compliment," Ianna snarks.

We've been driving by starlight for an hour, relying on the Beast's automatic guidance system to navigate. It's just the three of us in the cab, with Knott stationed in the back and Rust out on the flank on Akona.

The scablands are dark and moonless for the moment. Hera is a faint pink glow on the horizon, and her blue brother, Eros, set about an hour ago. We'll be moving at night until we get past the Guardian's battle lines. Hopefully we can slip through unmolested.

"Don't be so sure," Shadow shoots back. "I've known some thumpers who would be tickled to be called Horrors."

Ianna purses her lips. "I don't think that counts. Just because you're happy being called something terrifying, that doesn't make it a compliment."

"Sure it does. It's a compliment from their perspective. They want people to be terrified of them."

Ianna makes a sour face and turns to the window. Shadow smirks.

"Keep an eye on those two," Jmini says in my earcone. "I believe there may be a power struggle brewing."

I sigh and subvocalize my response. "I thought males were the ones who needed to make displays of dominance."

"Oh no. Alpha females are every bit as prevalent, they simply get talked about less. But if you look at any unit, the alpha female is usually obvious."

"So Shadow and Ianna both want to be the alpha?"

"It's too early to say for certain, but they do seem to be trying to establish a pecking order."

"Isn't breaking through the battle lines trouble enough? Why can't we focus on one problem at a time?"

"Humans are wonderful multitaskers."

"Ha-ha."

I gaze out the window, wishing I were out riding the flank with Rust. I'd kill to have my gravbike back. It's funny how you can miss people so much, but when you're stuck in a truck with them for hours, all you can think about is how you'd rather not be there.

Maybe there's something wrong with me. I spend years searching for my sister, and when I finally get her back, I don't want to be near her? That can't be normal.

Shadow pulls me back to the present. "So, how did Rust tame that Horror, Twist?"

"According to him, he didn't. It saved his life."

Ianna snorts. "Come on, Twist. That's a load of dust. Horrors don't save people."

I look out at Akona running through the darkness, sure-footed as a cliff-toe scaling a canyon wall.

"Well, this one did. She saved me, too, after Dad died."

"Uh-huh."

"I'm telling you, it's true. I wouldn't be here without her."

"If Horrors are so great, why have we been fighting them for a hundred years?" Shadow asks. "Why do they keep attacking us?"

"We attacked them first." I tell them about the greicagins, and how the first-expedition scientists hid the fact that the Hubzoh were intelligent.

"So they're just another victim of the IEC's greed? Why am I not surprised?" She cocks her head at me. "Do you think Julius knows?"

My jaw clenches at Julius's name.

"If he does, I'm sure he doesn't care. Exploitation and murder are business as usual for Julius Carlyle."

"Another reason he needs to die," Ianna growls.

"He killed our dad, kept you as a slave, and is in the process of slaughtering the Outsiders. I think we already have all the reasons we need," I say.

Shadow yawns and stretches, her jaw cracking. "Well, with that pleasant bedtime story, I'm going to get some shut-eye. Wake me up if anything interesting happens."

She curls up on the bench and rests her head on her arm. She's asleep in seconds.

Ianna shakes her head. "It must be nice, being able to sleep like that."

"It's a trick you pick up in Merrimac," I say. "The tests come at you without warning, all hours of the day and night. You learn to grab your z's when you can."

"I think I learned the opposite at the Carlyle estate. I can't remember the last time I slept more than a couple of hours."

I shift uncomfortably, trying not to imagine the things that might have happened to her. I steel myself to ask, but she changes the subject first.

"I can't believe you went to Merrimac."

"It was the only way I could think of to find you." I latch onto the more comfortable topic. Maybe it makes me a coward, but I don't really want to know everything that happened to my sister while Julius had her. I feel guilty enough for losing track of her. Details would just make it worse.

"You always did have your own way of going about things, Twist.

Only you would decide that winning the Guardian Tournament was the path of least resistance."

"Least resistance? Hardly. Winning my way through Merrimac was the most difficult thing I've ever done."

"So why did you do it?"

"I told you. I did it to find you."

"Come on, Theo. This is me you're talking to. You never cared that much about me before."

"We were just kids, Ianna. Maybe I didn't show it much, but that doesn't mean I didn't care about you. When you're around someone every day of your life, it's easy to take them for granted. Then one day Dad was dead and you were gone. When you're all alone in the world, you realize how important your family is."

She looks at me skeptically. "Well, whatever your motivations were, thank you for getting me out. Another year and they probably would have made me start popping out kids." She shudders.

"Why? Couldn't the slavers catch more street kids?"

"Yes, but then Julius would have to pay for them. Why buy kids when you can grow your own?"

"That's sick."

"That's life, Theo. Money rules everything. You said it yourself: It's the whole reason humans are on this planet. It's the reason our grandparents were shipped to Greica. It's the reason the IEC has declared war on an intelligent alien species."

"But Julius has plenty of money already, doesn't he? Why does he need more?"

Ianna looks at me like I'm an infant. "People like Julius will never have enough money, Twist. It's all a big game as far as they're concerned. They want to win all the prizes, and as long as they think there are more prizes to win, they'll keep playing."

"I just don't understand." I look out at the blue-white stars, the pink moon glow beyond the horizon. It's so beautiful and peaceful. "There's so much of everything. More than we could ever need. We can't we all just share it? Why do we have to fight over everything?"

"I don't know, Theo." Ianna sighs. "I wish I did."

11

The monsoon clouds break with the dawn, giving way to a bright, cold morning. My dad would have called it "sun with an edge." My eyes burn as I squint against the glare. We've been driving all night, and I'm hoping for a big cave where we can stop to wait out the day.

The Guardians have other plans.

"Drones at four hundred meters," Jmini snaps in my earcone, lighting up the intruders on my display.

"Spines. Look alive, everyone. We've got company."

"Shoot them down?" Knott asks.

I chew my lip. "If we open fire, we declare ourselves hostile. If we don't, maybe there's chance they'll think we're friendlies?"

Shadow snorts. "Keep dreaming, Twist. Knott, blast those little spies out of the sky now."

"Too late." Rust's voice is remarkably calm. "Gravbikes incoming."

At the far end of the canyon, a phalanx of gravbikes speeds into sight, headed right for us.

"Six riders. One thousand meters and closing." Jmini posts the tactical data on my display. Blue numbers tick down as the gravbikes close.

I'm technically sitting in the driver's seat, but that makes no difference. The Beast is fully automated, and Jmini's linked up with the massive truck's systems in case we need to take manual control.

I pull out my cannon and pop open the roof hatch, standing on the front bench seat so I can lean my elbows on the roof of the cab for stability. Shadow does the same on the passenger side, while Ianna leans out the window in the back. I realize with a guilty start that I don't even know if my sister knows how to fire a cannon. At least she's pointing the right end in the right direction.

The dull whump of Knott's twin-cannon hits my ears as she blasts the drones from the sky. Probably an empty gesture at this point, but at least they won't keep sending data on our position.

The gravbikes fan out so we can't take them out with a single area bomb. We don't actually have that capability, but they don't know that. Two bikes head toward Rust, the rest swoop down on the Beast.

It's bizarre watching the silver-armored forms rocket toward me— like looking in a funhouse mirror, and I've somehow become the distortion. Those Guardians out there are all I ever dreamed of being. When I close my eyes, that's still how I see myself: spotless and sleek, bent low over the gravbike's chassis, the rocky ground a crimson blur beneath me.

Hard to believe I'll never be that person again. I'm an Outsider now. A rebel. My dream came and went so fast I hardly had time to enjoy it.

Then the Guardians open fire, and the time for idle thoughts is over.

Knott's cannon whumps, scattering the riders like flitbats. I squeeze off a few shots, but only get puffs of dust for my trouble. The gravbikes are moving fast, locked into evasive patterns. Good luck hitting that.

I keep firing, though. As long as they're busy dodging our shots, they can't target the Beast effectively either.

Out of the corner of my eye, I see the two riders streak past Rust, flanking Akona. Rust does something too fast to follow, sending one of the riders tumbling over and over in the dust, their gravbike streaking on without them. I shake my head in admiration. Captain Steel hasn't missed a beat.

Something bangs against the door. I look down and realize one of the Guardians has latched onto the side of the Beast. I hear another bang onto Shadow's side of the cab. We're being boarded.

I lean over and squeeze off a couple of cannon blasts, but the Guardian's armor shrugs it off. I guess it's time to get personal.

I duck down inside the cab and draw my warpknife, the energy of the blade humming up through my arm. The climbing Guardian's head appears in the window. She's grinning, expecting to face a truck full of under-equipped Outsiders. Her eyes grow wide as I thrust my warpknife at her face.

The Guardian ducks out of sight, leaving my warpknife to take a chunk out of the window frame instead. Then she pops back up and tosses a small metal sphere into the cab.

"Grenade!" Jmini and I shout simultaneously.

The sphere lands on the bench seat next to me, blinking through the end of its detonation sequence. In my blind eye I see the energy build, a tiny sun about to go nova. I don't think, I just I throw myself onto the sphere.

The roar is deafening.

The explosion picks me up and slams me into the roof of the cab. Then gravity pulls me back down, and I crash headfirst onto the floor, my legs splayed out over the bench.

"Ow." I gingerly flex body parts, trying to assess the damage. My armor may be nearly impenetrable, but inside it, I'm still soft and squishy. Everything hurts, but I don't feel any of the sharp pains of broken bones. Small favors.

Jmini clears his throat. "I hate to interrupt your nap, but that Guardian is climbing in the window."

I turn my head and sure enough, there she is, slipping inside the cab. She squats on the bench beside me, her warpknife glowing yellow in her fist. She frowns at my black Guardian armor.

"Where did you get that armor?"

"Same place you got yours." I untangle myself from the floorboards and turn to face her. My warpknife buzzes green.

Her brow creases. "I don't understand. Are you on a covert mission? Why didn't you identify yourself?"

I laugh. "Yeah, I'm on a covert mission. Top secret."

I launch myself at her, diving across the seat of the big truck. There's not enough room in here to get fancy. And besides, my everything still hurts from smothering that grenade blast. I want to end this fast.

She raises her warpknife in surprise, but she's missed the point of my attack. I'm not trying to stab her.

I brush her blade aside with mine and slam my forearm into her chest. I'm heavier than she is, and I've got momentum and the strength of my legs behind me. The window frame catches her behind the knees and her legs fold. Her eyes go wide with understanding, her arms flail … and then she's gone. Swallowed by the billowing dust behind the truck.

One down.

Cannon fire sizzles behind me.

I turn to find Ianna blasting away at the second Guardian, her shots deflecting off the mirrored surface of his armor.

Shadow has managed to keep him outside the cab, and he's clinging to the window frame with one hand, like some kind of demented cliff-toe. His other hand clutches his warpknife, which he uses to parry Shadow's thrusts. With my blind eye I see the power running through his armor. It looks like a stalemate.

I want to help, but there's no way for me to get around Shadow on the narrow bench. Then I have an idea.

I look again at the Guardian's armor, tracing the lines of power. They remind me of the flowing greicagin-lines I discovered when I was locked in that cell in the heart of the Mesa. When I interrupted those lines, I was able to unlock the door to my cell. Maybe I can do something similar with his armor?

I take a deep breath and try to block out the chaos and noise, to focus on the power flowing within the Guardian's armor. I find what seems to be a major artery, carrying power from the shard that sits at the heart of his breastplate. With an effort of will, I reach out and pinch it off.

The effect is immediate.

Shadow slices at her adversary. The Guardian tries to parry her attack, but his armor doesn't respond the way it should, slowed by the lack of power. Shadow's blade catches him in the shoulder. He cries out, and I think he's about to fall. But he grabs the window frame with his other hand, stubbornly hanging on.

Ianna's cannon blast takes out a plate-sized chunk of window frame around his hand.

Just like that, he's gone.

We stare at each other for a moment, panting in the sudden silence. I check the windows. It looks like Rust has taken care of his adversaries as well. He and Akona are bearing down on the Beast, all six of the Hubzoh's sharp feet churning up crimson dust.

I look for the last two Guardians, and find one of them far away, fleeing up the canyon. The other gravbike smolders closer at hand, apparently the victim of Knott's dual cannon.

"So much for getting through unnoticed." I flip up my visor and collapse down onto the seat with a groan. This mission just got a lot more dangerous.

12

———

The battle lines are not a line. The Guardian forces are spread out over several kilometers, tracking down Outsider communities and chasing them deep underground. Now that they're aware of us, it's going to be even harder to break through.

"I say we don't stop. Just barrel right past." Ianna occupies a flat rock, munching on lanbrush seeds. "If we move fast enough, maybe they won't be able to stop us?"

We're sitting around a fire inside a deep cave, hiding out for the day. Knott hums happily, sprinkling spices into a bubbling pot. Her hair is windblown from standing in her turret in the back of the Beast, sticking out in wild clumps.

A pang of sadness goes through me as I remember Fin's grey hair sticking out like that too. I wonder if I'll ever see my old mentor again, or if I even want to. I was so angry when I found out he lied to me, but now that Dad's dead he's probably the closest thing to a parent I've got left. I frown as I scratch around the bandages over my eye, my heart and mind at war. I'm not sure if I can forgive him, but I'm also not sure if I can afford not to. Maybe life is too short to hold grudges.

Shadow rolls her eyes at Ianna. "You should leave the planning to those of us who actually have Guardian training."

Ianna scowls. "Don't treat me like a baby. My life is in danger, the same as yours. I get a say."

"Do you want a say in how we fight too? Maybe you'd like to show me some new moves with my warpknife?"

"Enough!" I step between them. "This is not helping. If you two can't contribute to the conversation like adults, I'm going to send you both to bed without supper."

"I'd like to see you try."

"This isn't a game," I snap. "We all work together or we all die together. Is that plain enough for you?"

"That's exactly what I was saying." She tosses a handful of lanbrush shells into the dark and smirks at Shadow. "We all have to work together."

I throw up my hands.

"Never mind. If you want to waste time squabbling, go right ahead. I'll be outside if you need me."

A hundred meters up, the cave takes a sharp left turn. It opens up around the bend, the ceiling receding into a high vault. A faint circle of daylight outlining the cave's entrance can be seen in the distance. The black silhouette of the Beast looms between here and there.

I walk up to the massive vehicle, running my hands over the blast marks and cannon scars. How many Guardian patrols can it survive? It's a tough, armor-plated transport, but everything has its limits. Hit it enough times, in the right spots, and it will go down.

Footsteps crunch over the gravel behind me. Rust shines in the greicagin-sight of my blind eye. It's like the particles have completely infused his bloodstream.

"They look to you to lead them."

I scuff the dust with my toe. "I don't want to be in charge."

"The best leaders don't. Those who seek power are often the least qualified to hold it."

"But why me? Shadow is smarter than I am. Knott is stronger. Ianna is… well, I don't know what Ianna is anymore. Harder. More ruthless, maybe."

"None of those qualities make someone a leader. Leading requires a certain blend of skills. You either have it or you don't."

I turn to look at him—this old man who was once a legend.

"You were the greatest captain in the history of the Guardians. *You* be in charge."

"It doesn't work that way. The leader is chosen by the pack. The pack has chosen you. They wouldn't follow me even if you told them to." Rust smiles. "Besides, my day has passed. It is your time now."

"But I'm just a rockhead. I don't know what to do."

Rust seizes my wrist and holds my hand up in front of me. "Do you see the power running through your veins? You are not 'just' anything. You can tilt the balance of this war."

I stare at the tiny rivers of light flowing through me. Greicagin dust, powered by the shard in my collarbone. It's as if I've become a part of Greica itself, with the strength of a planet behind me.

I shudder and pull away from him, feeling very small and very large at the same time. "I didn't ask for this. Any of this."

"Some are born to greatness. Some have greatness thrust upon them," Rust says.

"And some have weird crimson dust running through their veins."

I tilt my head back and run my hands through my hair. I need a haircut; it's starting to curl down over my ears. I'll add that to the list of things to worry about if we survive.

I sigh and look into Rust's metallic-sheen eyes. "Fine. But you have to teach me everything you know about this power we have. If I'm going to use it, I'll need all of it. And I want dueling lessons. You're the greatest fighter in the history of Greica. Maybe you can teach me something that will help us survive this dust storm."

Rust holds out his hand. "Done."

I take his hand and he jerks me forward, flipping me over his hip. I thump onto my back on the sand.

"Ow. What was that for?"

"Lesson one: Be ready for anything."

"Oh, great. You're one of those teachers." I roll up into a crouch and brush the sand from my shoulders.

"One of those?"

"A sneaky cheat." I pivot and kick out, trying to sweep his leg.

He hops out of range and waggles his finger at me.

"I see you're a quick study. Not quick enough, though."

I grin as I stand. "Give me time, old man."

13

A carpet of clouds covers the stars, painting the night ink black. The Beast rumbles beneath me, all running lights extinguished. A shadow within the dark. Perfect for sneaking across enemy lines. I hope.

The scablands are a glowing topographical map, the dust of Greica shining clearly in my mind. My blind eye sees more clearly than my regular one ever could.

Shadow and Ianna are sleeping, their blanketed forms sprawled out on the wide bench seats. Rust and Akona are off scouting. Knott refuses to leave her turret in the back.

I'm quietly dictating a message to Kass. I miss her more than I expected. She's like a hole in my center—a hole that aches all the time.

There are so many things I never got the chance to say to her. Explanations and apologies. Things I could never find the right words for.

She was the only Sunriser who accepted me, who might have even loved me. And all I did was lie to her. The least I can do is wrestle my thoughts down into a message. Tell her how sorry I am things had to end this way.

Maybe I'll even get to deliver it someday.

I wipe my eyes with the back of my hand. It's strange that my blind eye still cries. I peel off the last of the bandages and peer at it in the mirror. The scabs have mostly fallen away, leaving a shriveled white orb in their place. There's no way I'll ever see through it again. Should I get the eye replaced? My greicagin sight has gotten a lot stronger since Julius took my eye. Maybe the two things are related. Maybe I should just get an eyepatch.

I chuckle bitterly. Who would have thought that being half-blind could be a blessing in disguise?

Knott's black silhouette looms in the rearview mirror, pulling me from my morbid thoughts. "Aren't you cold out there, Knott?"

"No. I have heat in my armor. It's very warm." Her voice sounds a little sad.

"Is something wrong?"

"I am thinking about my family. I do not know when I will see them again. *If* I will see them again."

"At least your family is still alive."

"That is true. I am sorry for your loss, Twist. Your father was a good man."

"Yeah." I see my dad's body lying on the bank of the river. Feel the weight of the smooth stones in my hands as I place them over his body. Julius did that. Julius killed my dad. He's going to pay for that. "Tell me about your family, Knott. We should be fighting for the living."

"My family all live together in a single spire. Every morning, my grandmother and grandfather make breakfast for the whole family. There is fruit and many cereals and yogurt and potatoes. Then we go to the greenhouses to grow food for Canyon City."

"How big is your family?"

"I have four grandmothers, three grandfathers, nine aunts, seven uncles, six brothers, five sisters, ten nieces, eight nephews, and many, many cousins. Twenty-two, I think? Twenty-three?"

I shake my head in wonder.

"You all live together? Isn't it crowded?"

"Yes, but not crowded in the way you mean. Crowded for my family means busy and happy. It means life is never too quiet, and you are never alone. You always have someone to talk to or ask advice.

Someone to laugh with or someone to cry with. When I went away to Merrimac, it was very lonely. I was very unhappy at first."

"But there were five of us sharing a room!"

"Yes, but I did not know any of you. And I was ashamed to talk to you. I thought you would not understand my accent."

"So that's why you never spoke. We thought you couldn't even speak Standard. Grab and I made those translation earcones so we could talk to you."

"Yes, I am sorry about that. I did not mean to mislead you. I was ashamed."

"It's OK. We got it all sorted out in the end."

I stare at the dark through the windshield, trying to imagine what it would be like to have a big family. After my mom died, it was always just me, Dad and Ianna. The three of us against the world.

I glance back at my little sister, curled beneath a thin blanket on the backseat. Even asleep, her brow is creased with worry, her jaw working. My teeth clench in response. It's just the two of us now.

"Do you miss them?" I ask.

"Of course. Very much."

"Are you … are you sorry you joined us?"

"No." Her response is firm. "I am here for my family. I am fighting to make Canyon City a better place for all of them. I am the only one in my family to become a Guardian. I am the only one with this power, this opportunity." She pauses, and I hear a smile creep into her voice. "Besides, you do not think I am the only one who is fighting? I have brothers, sisters, cousins … There are many who help the Outsiders."

"And you still became a Guardian?"

"A person's beliefs should not stop them from getting a good job. Me becoming a Guardian was good for my family. It is always good to have family with power."

"And now you've thrown that power away."

"Only temporarily." Shadow's voice cuts in, making me jump.

"Don't you know it's rude to listen to other people's conversations?" I say, annoyed.

"That's not what they taught me in Covert class. I'm always listening, Twist. You should know that by now." She sits up on the bench beside me and pulls the blanket up over her head and shoulders. "But that's beside the point. If we're going to take Canyon City, we're going to need a lot of help. The people inside the walls will have to rise up. Knott's family could help spread the word."

"Retake Canyon City? Don't you have to take something in the first place in order to retake it?"

She rolls her eyes. "Fine, we can drop the 're' if you're going to get pedantic."

"Semantics aside, how do you think we're going to take Canyon City? The Guardians are kicking our tails all over the scablands."

"You've got to plan long-term, Twist. Winning a war takes vision."

Jmini chimes in on the Beast's interior speaker.

"The cannons have their bowels full of wrath,

And ready mounted are they to spit forth

Their iron indignation 'gainst your walls."

I snort. "Jmini agrees with you at least."

"That's because he's smart. He knows what it takes to win a war." Shadow leans forward, peering into my face. "By the way, that dead eye is really creepy looking. You should get that replaced."

"Thanks a lot." I scrub my hands over my face self-consciously. "Creepy eye aside, can we focus on the present, please? We're a long way from taking the fight to Canyon City. Right now we need get through the Guardian's lines undetected. Is that too much to ask?"

Jmini clears his throat apologetically.

"I'm afraid it is, Capitan. We've got incoming."

14

J mini puts the intruders up on the Beast's windshield display, but I can already see them sparkling in my mind. A cloud of drones, moving fast. And beyond them…

Shadow curses softly. "Spines, they've got the whole canyon blocked off."

Less than a kilometer ahead, the walls of the canyon lean toward each other. A barricade of vehicles stretches across this natural bottleneck.

"I count four large vehicles and at least a dozen Guardians," Jmini reports.

I pull my helmet on and climb out the back of the cab. "Shadow, you're in command here. I'm launching our new gravbike."

The wind outside the cab cuts like ice.

"Spines, Knott. How have you been sitting out here this whole time?"

"I told you: heated armor. For me it's a day at the beach."

"Jmini, can I get some of that please?"

"Aye aye, Capitan."

I sigh with relief as my armor's padding grows warm against my skin.

"Oh yeah, that's good. Now let's get this gravbike moving."

I feel a twinge of guilt as I use the Beast's tailgate lift to lower the gravbike to the sand. We salvaged the bike from the raiding party that attacked us yesterday. Its original rider is dead, killed by our hands. I wonder if they had a big family like Knott, or a small one like me? How many people will cry when they never come home? Did I know them? Would I have recognized them if I passed them in the halls of the Mesa?

Last week, that could have been me. Just a grunt doing his job. Killed in the line of duty.

I shake my head as I swing my leg over the gravbike's saddle. I don't have time for those kinds of doubt right now. Julius is trying to exterminate the Outsiders. Innocent families are dying in their homes. Anyone fighting on their side deserves what they get.

Adrenaline surges through me as I goose the throttle and accelerate away from the Beast.

"Just me and my gravbike," I whisper. This is the way it should be.

"Don't forget about me," Jmini says.

The corner of my mouth quirks up.

"How could I forget about you, Jmini? You're a part of me now. We're inseparable."

"Unless you've got a good set of surgical tools."

I laugh.

"Right."

I lean low over the chassis, enjoying the familiar hum beneath me. The winter wind pushes at me, but doesn't penetrate the seals of my armor. I am a planet unto myself.

"What's our scan footprint, Jmini?"

"The stealth armor you stole when you escaped from the Mesa is practically invisible, but the heat signature of the gravbike is another story. When you lean over the chassis like that, your armor partially masks it, but you're a long way from invisible."

"Yeah, that's about what I figured."

I tilt my head back and check the sky. Most of the drones are heading toward the Beast, but there are a couple veering my way.

"Rust, are you out here? Do you copy?"

Silence hisses over the line.

"Dust storms. I don't know where Rust is, kids. We might be on our own for this one."

"Is good." The hum of Knott's dual cannon powering up underscores her voice. "More for us."

Right.

I examine the barricade blocking off the canyon.

"Shadow, steer for the gap between the two vehicles on the far right. I think that's our best shot at breaking through."

"Aye aye, Capitan."

"Hey, don't you start that too."

"What, only Jmini's allowed to be a pirate? Unfair."

I shake my head. Just what I need: more fake pirates.

The drones are tiny points of light against the cloud cover, like stars wandering too close to the planet. I wait until they're only three hundred meters away before opening fire.

The first drone becomes a shooting star—flaming wreckage plummeting to the dust. The second takes evasive maneuvers, bobbing and weaving around my cannons as it returns fire. I do the same, and we perform an erratic dance across the night, each trying to anticipate where the other will be next.

It hits me first, but the beam just glances off my armored shoulder. When I finally tag it in return, the drone is not so lucky. A second flaming wreck tumbles from the sky.

"Status, everyone?"

"It's pretty hot over here." Shadow's voice is strained.

"Much cooking," Knott agrees.

Sure enough, the Beast is surrounded by a swirling constellation of drones. Shadow and Ianna's cannons burn upward, but the drones dance around the beams, peppering the slower truck with snapdragon missiles.

As I watch, a snapdragon slams into the left side stabilizers, causing the Beast to veer sharply. Knott is nearly thrown from her turret on the back of the truck. She dangles from the dual cannon by one hand, cursing like a monsoon.

"Hang on, I'm on my way." I lean low and throttle up hard, rocketing across the canyon floor. Unfortunately, I'm not the only one headed that direction.

"Dozer incoming, Capitan," Jmini says.

"I see it."

The dozer looms against the night, so big it makes the Beast look like a shellbaby. Shadow's never going to get past that thing, especially with her attention on the drones.

I veer to intercept the dozer, launching a flight of missiles. Half a dozen tiny fireballs bloom against its armor. The dozer plods right through them. I might as well be hurling handfuls of gravel at it.

"We need a better plan, Jmini."

"Aim for the heels."

"The heels?"

"Didn't they teach you anything in that school? Remember the way they bested Achilles. Find the monster's weak spot."

"Good idea."

As I close on the dozer, I focus with my blind eye. The power structure of the vehicle comes to life, thick lines of energy flowing like blood beneath its armored shell. They gather in three key points. Hit one of those, and I'll cripple the dozer.

The front of the thing is impenetrable, covered by a massive steel scoop. But other spots are not as well covered. Particularly the undercarriage.

"You didn't pack any mines, did you?"

"Mines?" Jmini sounds confused. "As a matter of fact we've got two. Why do you ask?"

"I'm going to stick them where the sun doesn't shine."

15

Four hundred meters to my left, the Guardians' barricade stretches across the canyon. It's strangely silent over there. Maybe they're all hunkered down, waiting for us to get closer.

To my right, a cloud of drones drops missiles on the Beast, dancing around the defensive cannon fire of my friends like simflies circling a carcass. But I can't help them right now; I've got bigger horrors to handle.

I'm bent low over the gravbike, flying toward the dozer. I've got to come at it from the side, get in behind that massive front scoop. But to do that I have to circle around it, and I don't have much time. The dozer is going to hit the Beast in less than a minute.

"Impact in fifty-two seconds," Jmini confirms.

"Shadow, you've got incoming." I yell over the roar of the wind against my helmet. "You might want to turn."

"I'm a little busy right now, Twist," —an explosion on Shadow's end garbles the sound for a second— "help us out here?"

"On my way," I growl, pushing the throttle all the way forward. This is going to be close.

"Forty seconds. Thirty-nine."

The crew of the dozer finally becomes aware of me, and a cannon swings my direction. I ignore it and keep pouring on the speed. No time for evasive maneuvers now; I just have to pray my armor can handle a direct hit.

"Twenty-seven. Twenty-six."

The cannon kicks up dust around me, but none of the blasts connect. My stealth armor must be throwing off the targeting AI.

The dozer looms up before me, a dark wall of metal. Its undercarriage sits about a meter and a half off the ground. Which is nice and high, but not high enough to ride beneath. In order to place the mine where I want it, I've got to get creative.

I hit the brakes and slew the gravbike into a sideways skid, extending my back hand and knee to keep me from pancaking into the dust. I slide beneath the undercarriage of the dozer, the hot metal so close I can smell it. As I skid beneath the hot spot where the dozer's power lines converge, I slap the mine upward. The grey disc maglocks onto the metal with a hollow clang.

Then I'm out the other side, sliding away from the massive vehicle. I fight to get my gravbike back under control. Throwing it into a high-speed skid is one thing, pulling it out of that skid is another.

Then the mine goes off, and I'm not worried about the skid anymore.

The force of the explosion lifts me off the gravbike and slams me into the dust. The air huffs out of me as I tumble across the hard ground, rocks and gravel pinging against my armor. Finally, I slide to a stop. I lie on my back, staring up at reflected cannon fire flickering across the cloud ceiling. I'm afraid to move. I don't want to know how many bones I've just broken.

A silhouette steps into my view. A man wearing antique armor.

"Need a hand up?"

I stare at Rust's extended hand dubiously.

"I don't know if I'm ready to move quite yet."

"Come on, don't be such a whiner. It was only one dozer."

"Only one?" I splutter with indignation. Then I notice his smile.

"You did well, Twist. Come on. Let's leave this place."

I let him pull me to my feet and cautiously test my body, wincing as a sharp pain stabs me in my side.

"Not as bad as I was expecting. Maybe just a cracked rib or two."

Rust sighs and shakes his head.

"Kids. You all think you're indestructible because you heal so fast. In my day, we took better care of ourselves."

"Speaking of taking care..."

I look around for the Beast and find it rumbling forward a couple hundred meters away. Only a few drones remain; the rest have presumably been burned from the sky.

But now they've got a new problem. The Beast is almost to the barricade.

"Spines. They're going to get chewed to pieces. We've got to help them break through. Jmini, where did the gravbike end up?"

Rust puts a restraining hand on my arm. "Relax. The barricade has been taken care of."

I stare at him as comprehension dawns.

"So that's where you disappeared to. You were clearing the barricade. And here I thought you were slacking off."

Rust looks indignant.

"Slacking off? I'd like to point out that you were just lying here on the ground when I arrived."

I grin. "Fair enough."

Akona comes up behind him, stepping daintily on her sharp feet. Rust cocks an eyebrow at her. "Want a ride?"

My gravbike glides up beside her.

"No thanks. I've got my own."

The barricade is eerily silent as we pass through, the vehicles that form the blockade silent and empty.

"Where is everyone?"

Rust points to a small cluster of tents near the base of the cliff.

"They won't be getting up anytime soon."

I wince, picturing him murdering Guardians in their beds.

"Did you kill them all?"

"No, I did not kill them all. Most of them are tied up in their tents. I'm not a monster. But this is war, Twist. Sometimes you have to kill them before they kill you; that's the way it works. I didn't see you hesitate when you blew up that dozer."

"Yeah, but they were attacking us. That's different."

"Is it? The soldiers in those tents would have attacked us too if given the chance."

I sigh. "I know. It just doesn't feel right, that's all."

"Killing people never feels right, Twist. If it does, there's something wrong with your head. Remorse is good. Remorse means you're still a functioning human being."

"So you regret killing them?"

"I feel remorse for killing them, yes. But I don't regret doing what needs to be done." He clicks to Akona, and the Hubzoh steps away from the ruins.

I wonder how many people Rust has killed in his life. I wonder if killing gets easier with time.

I shake my head and goose my throttle. We've got a long road ahead of us still. The Forsaken are waiting.

16

It takes three days to reach the Forsaken's territory. Even though we're technically outside Guardian territory, we keep to our schedule of traveling at night. Anything can happen out here in the wastelands between cities. It's better to be safe than dead.

During the day we hole up in caves, stretching our road-weary limbs and getting what rest we can. Knott keeps us fed. Shadow keeps our perimeter secure. Ianna disappears for hours at a time, wrestling with her private demons. I worry about her, but she pulls back every time I reach out to her.

Knott tells me to give her time.

"My sister is the same. Like a shellbaby. Always pulling away. She will come out at her own pace. Be patient."

I know Knott's right, but it's hard to be patient. I've been searching for Ianna for three years. Now I've finally found her, but she's still missing. I miss her. I want my little sister back.

Patience is not my strong suit, but I try. Every day, I try.

It helps that Rust keeps his promise to train me. We spend hours sparring, sweating out my anxiety, pushing my body until I collapse into pleasant exhaustion.

Rust is the best bladesman I've ever seen, better than the top-ranked duelists. I thought Instructor Asa was good, but the simplicity of Rust's movements makes her cuts and thrusts look clumsy in comparison. He's over twice my age, but during our sessions he never even breaks a sweat, while I drown in it.

"It's all about balance," he tells me.

I'm sprawled on the cave floor, picking sand out of my teeth for the hundredth time.

"Balance and anticipation. You need to know where your opponent is going to move, even before they do."

"Dead simple. Are you going to teach me to read their minds next?"

He cocks his head at me the way Akona does when something unexpected catches her eye. He presses his lips into a line.

"Now that you mention it, the two things are not unrelated. Perhaps we've been going about this wrong. Put your warpknife away. Come sit with me."

He lowers himself onto a flat rock, folding his legs smoothly beneath him. I clamber onto another rock, facing him.

"I want you to consider the flow of power within everything. The greicagin dust that saturates everything and everyone on this planet. I know you can see it as well as I do. It's what allows us to communicate with Akona, among other things. Take a moment and center yourself. Breathe. Close your eyes and find the power flowing within you."

I do as he asks, closing my eyes and focusing on my breath the way Instructor Skinn taught me back in Merrimac. In and out. Feeling the cool air pass over my teeth and my tongue, moving down my throat to fill my lungs.

My attention moves from my throat to my collarbone and the shard embedded beneath my skin. It pulses like the heart at the center of my nervous system. Except this system isn't composed of nerves and tissue, muscle and bone. It's composed of pure energy.

The energy moves in and out of the shard, circulating through my body like blood. Making my limbs glow.

The flow is bright and sharp through my blind eye, as if half of my brain has become attuned to the greicagin's frequency.

"OK," I say softly. "I've got it."

"Good. Now turn your attention outward, follow the pathways of the power. Let it lead you to me."

I do as he asks. I'm unsurprised to find Rust shining just as brightly as I am.

"Does it ever fade?" I wonder, looking at the tiny star of his own embedded shard.

"Yes, but it takes many lifetimes. That's why greicagins are so valuable. Why the IEC was willing to risk so much to get them. They ship them all over the galaxy, supplying virtually unlimited energy. At a very healthy profit margin."

"I imagine it is, considering all the free labor they have."

Rust inclines his head.

"Just so. But we are not here to talk about the IEC. We are here to talk about power. Focus on the power flowing through me. Tell me when you have it clear in your mind."

"I have it."

"Excellent. Now I want you to notice what happens when I do this."

His right arm grows brighter, the power concentrating and flowing in that direction.

I suck in a breath. "What did you do?"

"What did you see?"

"I saw your arm grow brighter."

"And why was that?"

I take a moment to think about my reply.

"It grew brighter because the power of the greicagin shard moved in that direction."

"And why did it do that?"

"I don't know," I admit.

"Shift your attention back to your own arm. Have you got it?"

"Yes."

"Now don't actually move your arm, but think about reaching out with it. Think about grasping your warpknife and holding it in front of you."

"But don't actually move it?"

"No. Only imagine the action."

I do as he says, visualizing my fingers wrapping around the hilt of my warpknife. As I think about extending the knife in front of me, a strange thing happens.

"The power is flowing into my arm!"

"Yes. Just as your brain sends impulses that cause your muscles to flex, it also communicates with the shard. The shard sends power to the part of your body that needs it. In this case, your arm. Now think about moving your other arm."

I do as he says, and watch the power flow to my other side. "Amazing."

"Now, to return to the original question. Why did the power flow to my arm?"

"Because you were thinking about moving it."

"Yes. Now, how might you anticipate where your opponent is going to attack?"

My mouth falls open.

"It can't be that simple."

"No, it is not," Rust concedes. "It takes practice and focus to identify movements within the fractions of a second you have to react when you are fighting. But if you work at it, you will master the skill in time."

"It feels like cheating."

"There is no cheating in battle. There is only winning and losing."

17

On my way back to camp, I hear a guitar somewhere deep in the cavern. I follow the sound to a small chamber lit by a single lamp. A wavering voice sings a song so sad and eerie it makes the hair rise on the back of my neck. The voice belongs to my sister.

As the last notes fade away, I step into the light.

"That was beautiful."

Ianna jerks as if waking from a trance. Then she scowls.

"It wasn't for you. Why do you think I came so far from camp to play? What are you doing here? Did you follow me?"

I hold up my hands.

"No, I just heard the music and followed the sound. I didn't know it was you until I got here. I'm sorry. I didn't mean to interrupt."

She glares at me doubtfully, her fingers idly plucking notes from the guitar. It's a strange-looking thing, little more than a neck with strings. I nod toward the instrument.

"Where did you learn to play that?"

"At the Carlyle estate. It's the only good thing that came out of that place."

"Where did you get it? You didn't have it with you when we escaped."

"I found it in the Outsider complex; someone had left it in a pile of extra gear. An old woman told me the original owner died." She looks down, running her fingers over the thin instrument. "It's a backpacker. Much smaller than a regular guitar. Perfect for a traveling minstrel."

I shift from foot to foot watching her pet her guitar. A minute ticks by and she doesn't look up.

"So you learned to play at the Carlyle estate?"

She nods.

"There were a bunch of children there. I was pretty good with them, so I was assigned to the school a lot. Sometimes we would sit in a circle and sing songs."

"I saw you," I say softly, remembering the vid. "Grab hacked the estate's security system and found footage of you doing a puzzle with the kids. It's how we knew you were there for sure." I don't mention the second part of the vid. The part where Mrs. Slate beat her bloody.

Ianna smiles sadly. "I miss the children. They helped keep me sane in there."

She falls silent, fingers stroking her guitar again. I don't want to ask, but I have to.

"What happened in there, Ianna? What did they do to you?" When she doesn't respond right away, I hesitantly add, "You said they were going to make you breed when you got older. Did they…?"

She shakes her head sharply.

"No, nothing like that. Not to me anyway. The guards would line us up against the wall sometimes and make a big show out of rating us. Judging our bodies like we were cattle. They took some of the girls, but never me. I guess I was too young and scrawny." She shrugs with one shoulder. "We were just things to them. Animals to be ordered around. If you didn't move fast enough, they hit you. If you messed up a task, they tasered you. If you spilled something, you had to lick it up off the floor with your tongue."

Her fingers have stilled now, her voice gone quiet and flat. I want to reach out to her, but I don't dare interrupt.

"I had a friend, a girl my age named Amber. She was the happiest person I ever met, always giggling for no reason, smiling and joking, making the rest of us laugh too. No matter how bad things got, Amber never stopped smiling.

"Mrs. Slate hated her. One night she dragged Amber out of bed and made her trim the hedges in the middle of the night. It was winter, and Amber was in her nightgown with bare feet. When she finally returned to the barracks, her lips were blue. She couldn't stop shivering.

"I pulled the blanket off my bed and piled it on top of hers, but Amber got sick anyway. She would cough for hours, her whole body convulsing beneath the blankets. I'd lie awake listening to this meaty, tearing sound, like she was hacking up pieces of her lungs.

"They could have helped her get better; they had medicine. But Mrs. Slate said being sick was part of Amber's punishment."

A tear rolls down my sister's cheek.

"They let her die. Die for some stupid punishment. That's how little we meant to them."

She pauses. I don't know what to say. Papa Grady's camp wasn't a nice place to live, but at least they tried to keep us alive.

"The night you broke into the barracks, I was ready to die. I'd had enough. That's why I attacked you when you came into the room. I was done being pushed around. Done keeping my head down and my mouth shut. I was so tired. I just wanted it to be over."

"I'm sorry," I say. "I'm sorry I didn't find you faster."

She looks up, her eyes wild. "I'm so angry all the time. I kept it locked inside for years, and now that it's started to come out, it won't stop. I want to hit them and kick them and beat them the way they did to us. If Mrs. Slate was in front of me right now, I'd bury a knife in her black heart."

Her hands are shaking, clenched into fists. They give me an idea.

"Do you want to hit something?"

"What?"

"Hit something. Work out some of that anger."

Her forehead creases. "I don't understand. Hit what?

"I don't know, anything."

"Do you really think that would help?"

"It might." I shrug. "It certainly can't hurt. Sometimes the only way to get something out is through your body. Burn the anger out."

Ianna looks doubtful.

"Don't say anything," I say. "Just stand up and hit me."

"Hit you?"

"Come on. You know you want to."

She eyes me for a moment, then sets her guitar aside.

"You're right. I do want to hit you."

She gets to her feet and raises her fists. I tap my chest.

"Right here. Hit me as hard as you can."

She tentatively taps me with her fist, and I chuckle.

"Is that all you've got? Do it again. Pretend Mrs. Slate's face is right here."

She hits me again, harder this time.

"That's better. Here, let me show you the proper way to punch."

I show her how to set her feet and make a tight fist. How to drive with her shoulder and pivot her hips, keeping her wrist locked.

After a few minutes of practice, she nails me hard enough to leave a bruise.

"Ow. OK, that's probably enough for one day." I rub my chest, grinning.

Ianna grins back, her eyes alight with feral satisfaction. For the first time since I pulled her out of the Carlyle compound, I feel I've almost got my sister back.

She quirks an eyebrow at me. "Same time tomorrow?"

I laugh.

"Sure. Same time tomorrow. But tomorrow I'm bringing some padding."

Ianna laughs too. The sound makes my heart soar.

"You'd better. You're going to need it."

18

The scablands change as we get closer to the territory of the Forsaken. The canyons become wider, the walls less steep. Instead of moving in a vertical maze, we're now traveling through open land dotted with broad mesas.

I look up at painted clouds strewn across the sprawling sky and shiver.

"It's so open here. It reminds me of Sunrise."

It's early morning and I'm out riding point on my gravbike. The Beast lumbers along half a kilometer behind me, while Rust and Akona guard the rear. We've decided it's better to move during the day now that we've left Canyon City's territory behind. There are no Guardian patrols to dodge out here, and if we run into any Forsaken, we don't want to be mistaken for raiders. So we move nice and slow, sticking to the wide-open spaces, visible to anyone who might be looking.

"This makes my skin crawl," I mutter.

Jmini tuts in my ear.

"You should learn to relax, Twist. Humans weren't meant to live underground. These wide-open spaces are your birthright."

"If this is my birthright, you can have it. I need tall walls around me. Give me a nice dark cavern anytime."

"You get used to it eventually, Theo," Ianna chimes in. "My first year in Sunrise, I hated going out to work the grounds. I felt like some giant flitbat was going to swoop down and carry me off. I'm not sure when I stopped being afraid of the sky, but I remember looking up one day and thinking, 'You know. This is actually kind of nice.'"

"Your mental damage goes deeper than we thought," I say. "We may have to operate."

Ianna huffs indignantly.

"I'm sorry to break up this little bonding session, but you need to look alive out there, Twist," Shadow breaks in. "We've got company."

Adrenaline shoots through me as I scan the horizon.

"Jmini?"

"Shadow is correct. There are a half … no, make that a dozen bogies incoming."

Red dots fill the grid map on my display. They're two kilometers out, and closing fast.

"Do you think they know we're here?"

"They know we're here all right," Shadow says. "They just shot down one of my drones and changed course. Now they're headed straight for us."

I curse. "Rust, you and Akona catch up to the Beast. I'm going to ride out to meet them."

"I don't think that's a good idea," Rust says. "The Forsaken aren't fond of visitors. We're safer staying together."

"Don't worry, I'm not going to go too close. I just want to get eyes on them and, more importantly, let them get eyes on me. I want to find out what kind of reception we can expect."

I mute my com and throttle up before anyone else can protest, putting distance between me and them. Rust has a point, but if they're going to put me in charge, that means I get the final say. And I need to see these Forsaken for myself.

I study the dots that represent the Forsaken on my retina display. It's impossible to tell what type of vehicles they're driving, but I can still tell a lot by what kind of formations they maintain.

In this case, that seems to mean no formation at all. The Forsaken are scattered across the display like flung gravel, changing positions without any rhyme or reason that I can see.

"Jmini, do you…" My words trail off as the dots disappear.

"They've shot down our last drone," Jmini says. "Would you like me to launch more?"

"No need. I've got this."

I focus through my blind eye, letting my mind move into my greicagin-sight. It expands outward, overlaying the topographic display on my other retina. Within moments, I've got the Forsaken's position back.

"We should see them when we round this next mesa. Be ready to broadcast, Jmini."

"What should I say?"

"I don't know, something soothing. Tell them we want to talk, and that we come in peace."

As I shoot out into the open, the dust plumes are obvious, spread out across the wide valley.

"Talk about a lack of military precision," I scoff. "There's over a kilometer between the front and the tail of their little welcoming committee."

"We're outnumbered four to one, Twist. Precision is less important when you have overwhelming force," Jmini reminds me.

"True. Are you broadcasting? Any response?"

"Yes, I am—and no, there is not."

I chew my lip, watching the plumes speed toward me.

"Keep it up, all frequencies. Let me know if you get anything."

I pump up the magnification on my retina display. I can just make out the leading edge of the oncoming force.

"Are those … What are those?"

The Forsaken vehicles are like nothing I've seen before. Blocky, asymmetrical monstrosities full of strange shapes and parts that look like they were welded on at the last minute. They seem to have been designed with no consideration for symmetry or aerodynamics, with chunky modules and cannons stuck on at random. They're hideous and unlike anything I've ever seen before.

"Why are their vehicles like that? They make my eyes hurt just looking at them."

"The Forsaken don't share human design aesthetics."

"Are you saying the Forsaken aren't human?"

"Not entirely, no. The Forsaken live in the wastes because they have embraced post-human technological upgrades. They are what you would call cyborgs."

"Like Grab?"

I picture my friend as I last saw him, permanently confined to his hospital bed, with thick wires burrowing into his empty eye sockets and blue fluid pumping into him through tubes.

"Not exactly. Despite his desire to become an AI, Grab has kept his human thought processes intact for the most part. The Forsaken have upgraded their minds to the point where they can seem quite alien."

"Does that mean they're AIs?"

"Some may be. They are not all the same. Each of them has achieved their current status through individual modification. There is no single definition that fits them all."

Wonderful.

I'd thought having Jmini in control was a significant advantage, but now I'm not so sure. If the Forsaken are cyborgs, some of them might be as fast as Jmini.

I slow and turn my gravbike perpendicular to their advance. I don't want them to think I'm charging into battle. Because I definitely am not. The oncoming vehicles bristle with more cannons than a reaper-plant has spines. I do not want to tangle with them if I can help it.

"Still no response, Jmini?" My voice cracks a little. My body thrums with tension.

"Negative, Capitan."

I chew my lip. In another thirty seconds they'll be close enough to start shooting.

"Send up a distress flare. Maybe if they think I need help, they won't try to kill me."

The flare goes up, arcing bright against the open sky. The Forsaken rumble closer. I can count the mouths of their cannons now. There are an awful lot of them.

"They'll be in range in ten seconds," Jmini reports.

I lean my gravbike away from the oncoming horde. "Maybe we'd better get ready to run."

On cue, cannon fire lights up the desert around me.

"Yup. Definitely running."

I lean forward and throttle up. My gravbike leaps like a spring uncoiling.

The Forsakens' cannons continue to fire, but their patched-together battle wagons seem designed for toughness, not speed, and I'm able to stay just out of range.

"What happens when we get back to the others?" Jmini asks.

"I don't know, Jmini. I think I'd rather not find out." I lean hard, bending the gravbike's trajectory into a long arc. Leading the Forsaken away from the Beast and Akona.

"So we're going to keep running? That seems counter-productive when we've come all this way to talk to the Forsaken."

I swerve as cannon fire puffs the dust a meter from my boot. My arcing trajectory has let the Forsaken close the gap.

"Give me a minute. I'll think of something." I hope.

Looking back at the bristling vehicles chasing me, I choke on a rising lump of fear. I can't say I like my odds.

19

"Do you want the bad news or the bad news?"

Jmini probably thinks he's being funny. I am not amused.

The Forsaken are still hot on my tail. I'm managing to stay out of range of their cannons, but just barely. They know this terrain a lot better than I do. Twice they've taken shortcuts that I didn't see, and almost cut me off. I can feel my time running out.

"Now is not the time to be clever, Jmini. Just give it to me."

The AI huffs.

"You've got to live every moment as if it were your last, Twist. If this is not the time to be clever, then when? If not us, then who?"

I swerve to avoid another cannon blast.

"Jmini! What do you have to tell me?"

"Fine. Spoilsport." The pout in his voice makes me want to bang my head against my handlebars. Who knew AIs could be so sensitive? "The bad news is some of the Forsaken have split away from the pack. They're now headed directly toward the Beast."

"Spines. So much for my distraction. And the other bad news?"

"The valley you are fleeing up ends in three kilometers."

My heart stutters.

"What do you mean, 'ends?'"

"I mean it gradually narrows until it ceases to exist."

My mind races. I push my sight forward, taking in the topography ahead of me. Sure enough, the valley closes down to nothing. Even worse, there don't appear to be any side canyons to escape into.

"Can you tell how steep the walls are? Can I ride out of it?"

"That's a negative, Capitan. To your second question, that is. The walls are over five hundred meters high, with a nearly vertical grade. The only way out of there is to fly."

"Wasn't I complaining about how open it is out here five minutes ago? How did I end up riding down the one valley that dead-ends into a box canyon?"

"Perhaps you are the victim of the old curse."

"Old curse?"

"Be careful what you wish for. You may just get it."

I take a deep breath, willing myself to be calm.

"Think, Jmini. There's got to be a way out of this. Are there any slot canyons I can wiggle through?"

"Negative, Capitan. Slot canyons may be a common feature in the scablands around Canyon City, but they are considerably less common around here."

"Spines!" I pound the handlebars with my fist. "There's got to be a way out!"

"I feel obligated to point out that we are running out of time. The canyon ends in one kilometer."

Even without consulting my mental map, I can see he's right. The walls of the valley have risen around us, narrowing to form a more proper canyon. The low morning sun hides behind them, and patches of overnight frost still cling to the shaded ground. The canyon is still almost a thousand meters wide, but the walls are closing in rapidly. If I'm going to do something, I'm running out of room to do it.

"Hang on, Jmini. Things are about to get interesting."

I lean hard and send the tail of the gravbike slewing around into a skid. Gravel pings off my armor, and the world disappears inside a rising cloud of dust. The bike wobbles, jumping my stomach up into my throat. I've oversteered, and I'm about to collect a face full of jagged rock.

Then I save it, wrestling the bike upright again and accelerating … right toward my Forsaken entourage. They applaud my maneuver by redoubling their fire.

"Twist?" Jmini's voice sounds more nervous than any AI's I've ever heard.

"The only way out of here is through them." I'm shouting over the roar of incoming cannon fire, dodging and weaving. "The longer we wait, the less room we'll have to maneuver. If we're going to do this, now is the time."

"That's not very reassuring."

"It's your own fault, Jmini. You're the one who convinced me to play Chaser after I pulled you out of the Crystal Clan's scrapyard. You made me ride a gravbike. I wanted to play Tank. Imagine how much armor we'd be wearing if we were a Tank right now."

Jmini sighs. "You have a singular talent for making me regret my life choices."

"Thanks. It's good to know our time together hasn't been wasted."

I yelp as a cannon blast sizzles off my thigh.

"Jmini, do you think you could take over the evasive maneuvers? These Forsaken gunners are getting a little too close for comfort."

"Oh, now you want my help. Fine. Lock down and hold on."

I lean forward and activate the maglock in my chestplate, clamping my armor to the gravbike's chassis. The second they connect, the gravbike goes crazy beneath me.

Jmini makes the bike veer and swerve so violently, I swear my teeth are going to shake loose from my skull. I hang on for dear life. If it wasn't for the maglock, I'd be rolling in the dust a hundred meters back.

His tactics are effective, though. The cannon fire can't track his unpredictable movements, and none of the shots are landing anywhere close. The only way one of them will hit us now is through blind luck.

Maybe we can survive this after all.

The Forsaken are spaced out across the valley ahead of me. Five of them. Breaking through their line might be harder than I thought.

Only one way to find out.

"Full speed ahead, Jmini. Our only hope is to slip this net."

"Aye aye, Capitan. Full speed ahead."

20

The gravbike leaps forward, slamming me against the inside of my armor. Again, I'm grateful for the maglock holding me to the chassis. At this speed, the wind alone might be enough to rip me from the back of the bike.

"How fast are we going, Jmini?" I croak.

"Only three hundred kilometers per hour at the moment."

"Only?"

"If we weren't performing evasive maneuvers, we could be going much faster."

Evasive maneuvers at three hundred kph. No wonder I feel like I'm being beaten with a jackhammer.

If we were facing humans, I'd be pretty confident right now. No way they'd be able to tag us at this speed.

But with the Forsaken, I don't know. I have no idea what their capabilities are. Maybe they can snatch a rider off a gravbike at three hundred kph. I hope not, but I have to admit it's possible.

The preliminary data looks good. Since Jmini took control, none of their cannon shots have been close. I pray the trend holds.

As we close to within one hundred meters, the first vehicle lets loose with a turret-mounted chain gun. Dust explodes all around us, and I can see spent shells raining down on the vehicle, metal casings flashing in the sun.

"Are they actually shooting slugs?" I hug the gravbike tight, willing my body to become a smaller target. Bullets puff the dust less than a meter from my foot. "Who does that?"

"They do, apparently."

Jmini's evasive pattern weaves the gravbike between the shots, but some of them are getting too close for comfort. Slugs are harder to predict than cannons, and hundreds of the little metal projectiles are coming at us, overloading Jmini's tracking system.

A slug ricochets off my shoulder and I flinch, the sound ringing in my ears like a hammer blow. Not good.

We're fifty meters from the lead vehicle. Forty. Thirty.

… and then we're flying past it, leaving the slugs behind in a cloud of crimson dust.

A fierce smile stretches my lips.

One down. Four to go.

The next vehicle has a big transparent tube sticking out its side, like a turret perpendicular to the ground. It looks like there's a copper coil inside it.

"What is that thing?"

"I don't know, but I think we're about to find out."

The gravbike starts to shake, tossing me around in my armor.

"What's happening, Jmini? Why is the bike shaking?"

"It's not the gravbike. The ground is trembling beneath us. I believe that thing is causing an earthquake."

"But we're suspended on a gravfield. We're not even touching the ground!"

"Be glad we're not. If we were, the tremor would have flipped us over. Even now it's threatening to destabilize our gravfield. I need to cut speed."

The shaking eases as we slow down, but that only brings up another problem. Cannon fire sizzles off my armor as the third vehicle comes into range.

"We're lined up like shellbabies. Evasive maneuvers!"

"I'm doing what I can, Twist. Maintaining our balance in an earthquake is extremely difficult. Performing evasive maneuvers on top of that may prove impossible."

"Manual control," I snap.

"I do not advise…"

"Manual control!"

Jmini huffs, but hands the gravbike back over to me.

The bike lurches sideways, nearly tearing the handlebars from my grip. Jmini wasn't kidding. Riding over an earthquake is no joke.

I lean hard, steering away from the tremor-tube. I've got to get past this thing before his partner burns me to a crisp.

The gravbike kicks and bucks like a trapped Horror; it's all I can do to hang on. Turning actually helps, letting me wrap my torso around the chassis as I put my weight into it.

Another shot burns off my side. My armor is deflecting the cannon, but if a shot hits the gravbike I'm in trouble. Ah, the joy of riding a gravbike. Most vehicles have armor to protect the driver. With a gravbike, the driver's armor protects the vehicle.

"I really wish you'd let me keep being a tank. Think of all the nice, thick armor I'd have on right now."

"If wishes were dart-rigs no one would ever walk."

"What?" A cannon shot sizzles across my back. "Stop distracting me. I need to focus."

The sniper vehicle swings out wide, angling for a better shot at me. The maneuver opens a slice of daylight between it and the earthquake-mobile. I can see the last two vehicles through it, spaced thirty meters apart. It's a straight shot to that gap, and freedom.

I grit my teeth and throttle down hard.

The gravbike leaps forward, pitching and bumping like I'm riding a rock-garden. A hard wave sends the bike airborne for a second, then slams us back to the ground. The bottom of the gravbike scrapes gravel, snapping my teeth closed on my tongue. The pain makes my eyes water, and I taste blood.

The gravbike slews to the side, fishtailing, and now my heart is in my throat, the ground rushing up at me. I start to go down.

Then the gravfield catches and, miraculously, the ground stabilizes. I'm past the earthquake generator.

"Eat dust!" I whoop, pumping my fist, grinning fiercely. Three down, two to go.

I aim the nose of the bike at the gap between the last two vehicles and throttle up, the wind pushing at me as I approach three hundred kph again. I'll be through the gap before they even know I'm there.

They both open fire, but evading them feels easy now that I'm past the earthquake zone. I shoot toward the gap, tasting freedom.

Final pass.

I'll be through the gap in three.

Two.

One.

A net springs up between the vehicles, filling the gap. My eyes widen … and I slam into it at three hundred kph.

The net wraps around the gravbike, pulling the nose down. We crunch into the ground, bouncing and rolling, kicking up a cloud of dust so high they can probably see it back in Canyon City.

I finally stop rolling and lie groaning in the wreckage while the world spins around me. My body feels like a drum set. Everything hurts.

After a minute, the net goes taut and I start to slide across the ground. Gears grind and complain as the Forsaken reel me in.

21

———

I'm lying in a bare cargo hold, tangled in the net and the twisted metal that used to be my gravbike, listening to the rumble of the Forsaken vehicle's engine echo off the bare metal walls. I'd probably be scared if I wasn't in so much pain.

My armor protected me from the worst of the crash, but doing a faceplant into the dust at three hundred kph did not feel good. I'm going to be one big bruise tomorrow.

I have to admire the Forsaken's strategy. Using the earthquake machine to funnel me toward that gap between the other vehicles. Netting me like a flitbat.

I don't like being on the losing end, but I can appreciate good tactics. Assuming I live long enough to appreciate anything.

"Do you know what happened to the others?" I carefully subvocalize to Jmini. No sense giving away my ace in the hole.

"Negative, Capitan. I've had no contact with the rest of the crew since we engaged the enemy."

"Well that's something, anyway. Maybe they got away."

"It's certainly possible. Though I wouldn't count on it. When the Forsaken greeting party split, the majority went after the others."

"Spines. Some rescue mission this turned out to be. I don't think we'll be bringing back those reinforcements."

"My calculations indicate the probability is quite low. Still, one can hope. While there is life, there is hope."

"Is that another one of your quotes?"

"Yes, Capitan. Attributed to Marcus Tullius Cicero, a Roman philosopher."

"Well, I guess our time here hasn't been completely wasted."

"Indeed, Capitan."

The sound of the engine drones on. Time smears and blurs. I think I pass out for a while.

The next thing I know, the cargo-bay door is opening, and bright sunlight is spilling in through the gap.

A steel bot enters the hold, clicking over the deck on spindly legs. It's got a human-shaped face, with wide, flat eyes and no mouth. It slices through the net with a laser implanted in its finger, which it then uses to free me from the wreckage of the gravbike.

"Thanks." I stretch my now free arms, wincing at the pain stabbing through my wrists and shoulders.

"You will come with me." The bot turns, obviously expecting me to follow it.

It hasn't bothered to disarm me, and I think about drawing my warpknife and making a run for it.

But where would I go? I don't even know where I am. And judging from the way my body creaks and protests as I lever myself up to my feet, I couldn't run right now if I wanted to. Maybe a zombie-like shamble, if I'm lucky.

No. My best play is to go along with it and see what happens.

I follow the bot out of the cargo hold and stop, amazed. We're in a large parking lot, in the middle of a broad, flat valley. Buildings rise on all sides of the lot, blocky structures several stories high. The walls have a pieced-together, salvaged look to them.

"Where are the spires?" I breathe.

"The Forsaken do not live inside of stone. They prefer to build free-standing structures," Jmini replies.

"A free-standing city?" I spin around in awe.

Canyon City doesn't have many free-standing structures; most of it is hollowed out of spires and mesas. But this place is out in the open—there are no spires to hollow out. Above us, the sky seems to stretch forever.

I reel and stumble back a step.

"This is how the Forsaken live? All the time? But why?"

The bot clicks a metal tether around my arm before Jmini can respond.

"You will come with me."

It steps forward, tugging at the tether. I have no choice but to stumble along behind.

It drags me to a squat building with rusted window frames. Inside, the bot pushes me into a small, open car set on a polished metal track. It clicks my tether to a rail on the side of the car and sits down next to me. The car carries us out into the city proper.

Jmini wasn't kidding about the Forsaken. Everywhere I look are cyborgs, ranging from seemingly normal people with robotic eyes to human faces mounted on inhuman steel skeletons. A hairless woman walks past, with a half-meter crest running down the center of her scalp and back. The crest is the color of a mandarin peel, and flexes gently as she moves.

"It's a heat sink," Jmini explains. "It vents excess heat from her core."

A man with steel treads instead of legs rolls past my other side.

"He reminds me of Grab," I say. "Before the accident, anyway."

In Canyon City, Grab was ridiculed for his metal legs. Shunned by the other Sunriser kids. Here, he'd be just another cyborg in the crowd.

The car delivers us to a long, low building with mirror-black walls.

"Solar collectors," Jmini says. "The Forsaken don't rely on greicagins for power the way we do. It's one of the main reasons they are allowed to live independently. If they were using greicagins, the IEC would see them as competitors, and treat the Forsaken the same way they treat the Outsiders."

"But isn't solar power inefficient?"

"Not particularly. It's less efficient than greicagins, but so is everything. The IEC narrative stresses how inefficient other forms of power are because they want to keep us dependent on greicagins."

I take in the technological marvels around me and scowl. How many of the things I've always taken for granted have been IEC propaganda? Could we have all been living out in the open like this if we'd wanted to?

Not that I'd want to. Give me a solid apartment in the middle of a stone spire any day. But still, it'd be nice to know what the possibilities are.

The bot leads me to a small room with a clear glass front wall.

"You will wait here."

"Wait for what?"

"For further instructions."

Well, that clears things up. I'm so glad I asked.

"We're here to talk to your leaders. We're looking for allies."

"You will wait here."

I sigh. Clearly, I'm not getting anything else out of the thing.

I step into the room and the bot unclips my tether as it slides the thick door shut behind me. The room is an empty square. White walls and a thin grey carpet. No chair, no bed, nothing. I turn and press my face against the clear front wall. The plexiglass is cool against my skin. I smell hot metal and lubricant.

Outside my enclosure is a wide promenade passing a hive of open-fronted shops. The whole place hums like a giant machine, and violet strips of light run along the ceiling of the hall.

Directly across from me is a dimly lit cube with chairs like those in a dentist's office. A huge projected pyramid floats in the middle of the room, with colored blocks moving in and out of it. A dozen Forsaken sit facing the projection, their skulls plugged into the chairs with thick bundles of black wire. I shudder. Grab would be right at home here.

Forsaken of all shapes and sizes hurry through the open space between me and the pyramid room. Many study the pyramid as they pass, but a few glance my way curiously.

"I feel like a zoo animal."

"You do smell like a goat," Jmini says.

"Funny."

I pace the square room for a few minutes, three strides each way. My hands clenched into fists as I remember the last time I was locked in a cell like this, back in the Mesa, before we rescued Ianna and fled to the scablands. The Guardians kept me locked up for days, and the inactivity almost drove me mad. I swallow the rising panic, trying to convince myself things will be different this time.

My fingers brush the sheath on my belt. "Why did they let me keep my warpknife?"

"I don't know. Perhaps they don't believe it will do you any good. There are hundreds of Forsaken here. One close-range weapon is hardly going to win your freedom."

I frown. "That's not very reassuring."

I make myself stop pacing and press my spine against the white wall. Sliding my butt down to the floor, I draw my legs up and clasp my hands around my knees. I think about Ianna and Shadow and Rust and Knott as I watch the bizarre Forsaken rush by. My fingers find the hilt of my warpknife. They'd better be OK. If they're not, these cyborgs are going to find out just how effective one close-range weapon can be.

The colored blocks move in and out of the pyramid across the hall in a hypnotic dance. I stare at them, feeling utterly lost. I'm even more out of my depth here than I was the first time I stepped into Merrimac. The Sunriser kids were strange, but at least they were still human. The Forsaken are something entirely new under the sun.

22

———

I've been sitting for hours when the bot finally returns. He's not alone.

I leap to my feet. "You're alive!"

My friends are a bedraggled bunch, their armor scorched and dusty. I hug Knott and Shadow as they shuffle in through the cell door.

"Alive. That's one way of putting it." Shadow backs into a corner, scowling.

"What happened?" I ask.

"They captured us, obviously." Ianna crosses her arms over her chest and claims the corner opposite Shadow.

"They made us look like children," Knott explains.

"Children may be exaggerating a bit," Rust says. "But it certainly wasn't much of a fight."

I shoot a questioning look at him. "Where's Akona?"

"She got away," he says. "I told her to run."

"Why didn't you run too?"

Rust's face colors.

"The Forsaken used some beam to lock up my armor, and I just fell off her back. In the moment, all I could think of was keeping her safe.

So I sent her away, while I lay there in the dust like some helpless shellbaby."

"Well I'm glad you're all safe. Did the Forsaken tell you anything?"

"No." Ianna scowls, her eyes flashing. "They just dumped us in this room like a bunch of children. They wouldn't answer any of our questions."

"At least we're all together now."

Ianna barks a laugh.

"Is that supposed to be a good thing? Hooray, we're all sharing a cell?"

"We're alive and unharmed," Shadow snaps. "If they wanted to kill us, we'd be dead. The fact that we're still alive means they have other plans."

"Great. Maybe they'll let me babysit their cyborg children." Ianna's voice rises. She pounds the glass with her fist. "Hey, freaks! We're not your pets. Let us out of here!"

"Yes, let's do more of that. I'm sure yelling will help," Shadow says acidly.

Ianna ignores her. "Hey! I'm talking to you! Let us out of this cage!"

"Ianna…" I reach out to grab her arm.

"Don't touch me!" Ianna retreats to the back of the cell and curls in on herself. "I was locked up for three years, Theo. I'm not going to be locked up again."

I squat down in front of her, maintaining a careful distance.

"We're going to get out of here, I promise. I'm not going to let you down again. Will you trust me?" I wait until she meets my eyes. "Good."

I stand and face the others.

"So, how do we get out of here?"

"The Forsaken captured us alive for a reason," Rust says. "They'll be back to fetch us soon enough.

"But what if they're not?" I press. "What then?"

"Can you do that trick with the cell door you did back in the Mesa?" Shadow asks.

"No. Their locks aren't powered by greicagins here, so I can't affect them."

She gets to her feet and crosses to the door, examining the locking mechanism.

"The good thing about a transparent door is you can see all the inner workings." Shadow bends down, bringing her eye close to the lock. "They didn't take my picks, so I'm pretty sure I could pop this if I needed to."

"Well, at least we've got an emergency backup plan. That makes me feel a little better." I sigh and run my hands through my hair. "Did the Forsaken talk to you at all? Did you tell them we were here looking for help?"

"We told them, but they did not answer," Knott says. "Maybe they did not understand?"

"Didn't understand?" I cock an eyebrow at her. "What do you mean?"

"Maybe they do not speak the language."

"Or maybe they weren't authorized to speak to us," Rust says. "If they have a strict hierarchical system, the drones may not be allowed to speak for their masters."

Shadow perks up.

"Drones? Are you saying the grunts aren't autonomous?"

Rust waggles his hand.

"I'm saying it's possible. The ones that brought us in didn't have a lot of personality."

"Interesting theory." Shadow steeples her fingers. "Do you think they're remote-controlled? Or do they just have a limited menu of actions they can perform?"

"If my theory is correct, I'd say the latter. Remote control seems hopelessly clunky."

"Yeah, that's why the Guardians have stopped using HAMRdroids outside of Canyon City," I say. "It's too easy for the signal to be blocked or lost."

"So we just got captured by a bunch of bots with limited intelligence? My confidence in this mission is growing by the second." Ianna scrubs her face with her hands.

"Hypothetically," Rust reminds her. "It's all hypothetical at this point."

Ianna snarls. "We know! Hypothetically, we're going to ask the Forsaken for help. Hypothetically, we'll keep the Outsiders from getting slaughtered. Hypothetically, we won't starve to death or die of old age in this room!"

Everyone stares at her, silenced by her anger.

I say, "Maybe we should all take five. Cool off for a minute."

Shadow smirks at me and rolls her eyes, but thankfully says nothing. Ianna wraps her arms around her knees, glaring at the colored blocks moving around the pyramid across the hall.

Pressing my forehead to the glass, I watch the Forsaken move past our cube. They're all strange angles and asymmetrical parts, weird glowing strips and gleaming gears. I've never seen anything like them. I've tinkered with a lot of bio-electronics, but I can't even begin to imagine how they function. They're like an alien species. I look at Ianna out of the corner of my eye, watch her follow the pieces inside the pyramid. She's got that crease between her brows she gets when she's absorbed in a puzzle, her mind identifying patterns and fitting pieces together in a way that's every bit as alien to me as the Forsaken outside our cube.

Since I pulled her out of the Carlyle estate, it's like there's no normal human temperature in her; she flips back and forth between icy logic and searing anger. Less than three meters separate us, but she might as well be a million kilometers away. I sigh and turn back to the glass, wondering how my own sister became so indecipherable.

23

———————

A cyborg with a black carbon face opens the door to our cube. His body is humanoid in shape: a patchwork of dark flesh and gleaming machine, with heat sinks spiking out from his skull like porcupine quills. His electric-blue eyes lock onto us.

"I am Spanner. Come with me, the council awaits." He walks away without waiting for a response.

Shadow meets my questioning look with a shrug. "Have you got a better option?"

We follow Spanner down the wide promenade. The Forsaken complex is shabbier than I expected, with rusted metal patching over gaping holes in the walls and bundles of exposed wires running along the ceiling.

"It reminds me of the Outsider caves," I say quietly.

Shadow nods.

"That makes sense. The Forsaken are to Sapphire City what the Outsiders are to Canyon City."

Ianna snorts. "Are they? I don't hear any bombs falling."

Shadow looks annoyed, but keeps her voice calm. "They've been more successful in their bid for independence. The Sapphire City people mostly leave them alone."

"Why is that?" I wonder.

"The Forsaken have become something other than human," Rust says. "Perhaps they've transformed themselves so much Sapphire City doesn't want them back."

I eye our cyborg guide dubiously.

"So the key to Outsider independence is to give up our humanity? I don't know if it's worth it."

"Don't think of it as giving up. Think of it as moving on to the next stage of evolution." Shadow indicates a metal-hipped cyborg striding by in the other direction. "Look at how smooth that steel is. Think about how much easier life would be without those floppy bits getting in the way."

I shudder.

"I think I'd rather keep my floppy bits."

Spanner leads us into a large room with a raised dais at one end. On the dais, six cyborgs sit behind a curved black table. Our guide joins them, bringing their number to seven. There are no chairs for us, so we stand awkwardly in front of the table.

I'm surprised to see a multi-colored pyramid projected in the air above them. It looks just like the one across the hall from our cell. I shift my gaze to Ianna. Sure enough, her eyes have locked onto the pyramid like an imfalcon sighting prey.

The cyborg seated in the center of the table speaks. Her head is gleaming metal, shaped so perfectly it looks like a human face that's been dipped in molten steel. Her eyes shine with emerald light.

"I am the Moderator. The council is now in session. Please state your business."

Everyone looks to me.

I hesitate, unsure what to say. This seems to be the audience we wanted when we came here, but the way we were captured and brought to it makes me uncertain. Do I start by flattering them? Do I come right out and ask for help?

I take a deep breath. Only one way to find out.

"Greetings. Um, thank you for seeing us. We've come a long way to talk to you."

I pause. The council doesn't respond. They don't even blink or nod to let me know if I'm on the right track. I swallow and push on.

"We are part of the Outsider movement of Canyon City. Like you, we are fighting for independence from the Guardians who control the city. Independence from the IEC." A few of the council members still have flesh faces, and I think I see a flicker of interest at this. I hope that's a good sign.

"Why have you come to us?" A man with a patchwork skull asks. There's a clear window above his left ear, about four centimeters square. Through it, his pink brain is visible.

His directness makes me hesitate again. It seems like they don't waste words around here. All right: If that's the case, neither will I.

"The IEC has launched an all-out assault on our people. They are trying to exterminate us. We have come to offer an alliance, and to ask for your help."

The council members stir in their seats.

"Why would we ally ourselves with you?" A blocky construct seated at one end of the table asks. It reminds me of the Forsaken vehicles that chased me down, with parts welded onto its torso seemingly at random. It has no head, and it's hard to tell where the thing's voice emerges from.

"Our goals are aligned," I reply.

"Are they? What do you imagine our goals to be?"

"Independence. Isn't that why you're living out here in the wastes? To get away from the IEC?"

"That is one reason," the construct concedes. "There are other reasons of equal importance."

"But without independence, our other goals cannot be achieved," Spanner pipes up.

"We already have independence," a tall, willowy cyborg says, her voice melodious as a flute.

"No, what we have is indifference," our former guide argues. "They are not the same thing."

"That indifference keeps us safe, Spanner," the slim cyborg retorts. "Getting involved in the humans' conflict will only draw attention to us."

"The IEC's attention will turn to us all, sooner or later." I say. "You can't avoid that fact by burying your heads in the sand. If we don't join together, they'll stamp the resistance movements out one by one. When your turn comes, you won't have anyone left to turn to for assistance."

"Are inferior allies worth having? Humans are not our equals," the Moderator says.

"This is a valid point." Spanner looks down at us with his electric eyes, black carbon face expressionless. "But the humans are numerous. Perhaps their numbers make up for their weakness."

"For years, Sapphire City has left us alone," the slim cyborg says. "And we have prospered. We should not disrupt that balance."

"What if they are only biding their time? Building their strength? What if they plan to wipe us out with one massive assault, as Canyon City is now trying to wipe out the Outsiders?"

The construct interrupts with a sound like gears grinding. "We have no evidence of that."

"When we do have evidence, it will be too late." Spanner's porcupine quills pulse and flex.

"We all know you want to attack the humans," the construct says. "You have put forth this argument for years."

I'm surprised to see the Forsaken arguing amongst themselves. I expected to plead our case, convince them to help us. Instead, it seems like we've brought an old argument to the surface.

"Force or money." A new voice joins the conversation, a large, spherical cyborg resting on the floor beside the Moderator.

It says nothing more, and the Moderator turns to it.

"Would you care to elaborate on your statement?"

"Force or money," the sphere repeats. Red light migrates across its surface. "These are the only things humans understand. We must have one or the other for them to treat us with respect."

"Are you proposing we trade with the humans, Eight-four-one?" The Moderator says.

"I am proposing nothing. I am merely stating facts. Historically, war or trade are the only outcomes when dealing with humans. They will not leave us alone forever. We must choose a path on which to move forward."

A thoughtful silence falls at the sphere's words.

"I never thought of it quite that way before, but the sphere raises a valid point," Jmini whispers in my ear. "As a species, humans do not leave their neighbors unmolested. Their fingerprints are all over everything they've ever come in contact with."

The Moderator speaks.

"We have many things to consider. Spanner, escort our visitors back to the holding cell while we weigh this matter."

24

———

"Well that was pointless." Ianna resumes her position in the corner of the cube, arms crossed over her chest. Her eyes fix on the projected pyramid. "I'm so glad we wasted all this time coming out here."

"They're thinking about it." I say, trying to stay positive.

"Thinking about it? Really? There were seven cyborgs at that table, and only one of them would even consider helping us."

"You don't know that. They weren't all speaking."

"I hate to agree with Little Miss Sunshine, but she's right. The cyborgs don't want any part of our war." Shadow leans against the clear wall. "I think we're on our own."

"Come on, anything is possible. Knott? Rust? What do you think?"

Knott shrugs and looks at her feet.

"It could go either way." Rust waggles his hand. "But we may have made a mistake coming here."

"Why's that?" I ask.

"We've been looking at the problem wrong. Trying to bring more troops into our fight, instead of making the best use of the ones we already have."

"The ones we already have are getting killed," Ianna scoffs. "That's the whole reason we're here."

Rust nods. "True. But they're also reacting, not acting. The Guardians are controlling the lines and picking the battlefields. The Outsiders could do better with a coordinated counterattack."

"This is a conversation you should be having with Tempest, not us," I say. "We already tried one counterattack when we tried to take out Julius inside Merrimac. It didn't go well."

"That wasn't a counterattack; it was a surgical strike. Which could still work. But I think it would have the best chance of success if it was combined with an overall counterattacking strategy."

"Why are you bringing this up now?" Shadow asks. "You could have saved us a lot of time by speaking up before we left."

"I didn't want to undermine Tempest's authority. And I still don't. But I think you could. You're the best-trained fighters outside the wall."

I snort. "No, we're not. You are."

Rust waves this away.

"I'm an old has-been. A crazy hermit with a pet Hubzoh. Nobody listens to me anymore."

"Why should we listen to you then?" Shadow asks.

Rust stops and looks thoughtful. "That is an excellent question."

Spanner appears outside our cell. His smooth carbon face betrays nothing.

"The council will not help you. We see no benefit in having inferior allies."

I step forward. "So you're going to send us home empty-handed?"

"That is doubtful. I believe you have seen too much to be allowed to leave."

My stomach drops. They're going to keep us here. Or kill us. Either way, we won't be bringing help back to Canyon City.

Spanner pauses as his electric blue eyes pass over Ianna. She's staring at the pyramid, her lips forming silent words. The cyborg steps between her and the pyramid, cutting off her view, forcing her to meet his eyes.

"You are wasting your time, human. You cannot hope to understand the pyramid; it is a puzzle that is constantly evolving. We use it to test ourselves against one another."

Ianna's eyes flare. "You know what they say about making assumptions. I bet I understand that pyramid better than you do."

Spanner laughs. "You humans are amusing. I will give you that much."

"I challenge you to a game." Ianna gets to her feet and crosses to the clear barrier, staring Spanner down. "If I win, you let us go. And you help us."

"You are not like other humans, are you?" Spanner studies her curiously before locking eyes with one of the Forsaken playing the game across the way. His head cocks as some invisible communication flashes between them, then his quills flex and his eyes find Ianna once again. "Very well, you may play. Perhaps we will find it amusing."

He opens the door.

I block my sister's path. "Ianna, what are you doing?"

"This Forsaken is an arrogant sot," she snaps. "Just like Julius. I'm going to take him down a peg."

My eyebrows climb my forehead.

"Really? You think you can step in and beat a cyborg in a game you've never played before? You calling him arrogant is like a lead bar calling granite dense."

"Just watch me." She shoulders me aside and steps out of the cube.

"Of course, if we are betting, winning and losing must have equal consequences." Spanner wraps his carbon fingers around the back of her neck. Ianna tries to pull away, but the cyborg holds her tight.

"Consequences?" she squeaks.

"You are asking us to risk our lives. In declaring war on the humans we would risk our entire civilization."

"What do you want?" Ianna holds herself still, every muscle locked. Her eyes meet the cyborg's without blinking.

I'm terrified and impressed. How can she face that thing without struggling? Looking at those fingers on her neck makes my skin crawl.

"If you win, we will assist you. If you lose" —Spanner uses his thumb to tilt Ianna's head to the side— "you will be harvested for parts."

"Parts?" I choke. "What does that mean?"

The blue eyes never leave my sister's face.

"Our biological components wear out and must be replaced. We are always in need of new parts."

I sway as his words hit me. It's the scrap vats all over again.

"Ianna, no," I shout.

My sister looks at me for a second. I see fear in her eyes, but it's nearly obscured by desperation and anger.

"They aren't going to let us go, Twist. If I don't do this, we'll probably be harvested anyway. At least this gives us a chance."

"No. You can't. There's got to be another way. Let me play, I'll go instead." Fingers of panic are wrapped around my throat, squeezing so tight I can hardly breathe. I didn't search for my sister all those years only to lose her now. I promised my dad I'd take care of her.

"I won't be a victim any more, Twist. I'm making my own choices. And I choose to fight." She lifts her chin and turns back to Spanner. "I accept your terms."

The cyborg's face doesn't react, but the tips of his quills darken to a deep red. Like they've been dipped in blood.

"Challenge accepted, human. Let the game begin."

25

Through the clear wall of our cage, we watch Spanner lead Ianna to the chairs surrounding the pyramid.

Shadow sidles up beside me. "How is she going to play?"

"What do you mean?"

"I mean, I don't see any haptic rigs. All the cyborgs have those thick bundles of wires plugged into their skulls."

I frown. Shadow's got a good point. Their game setup doesn't look very human-friendly.

Spanner straps Ianna down into her chair. Thick bands go around her forehead and chin, holding her head motionless. I hear the high whine of a drill. My sister starts to scream.

Hurling myself at the door, I shout. "Stop! You're killing her!"

I hack at the lock with my warpknife. The door is made of surprisingly strong stuff, and only comes away in little chunks. But I keep at it. Nothing can resist a warpknife for long.

Across the hall, Ianna stops screaming. Her hands grip the armrests so tight I can see the tendons standing out on the back of her hands. Her panicked eyes are darting around; for a moment, they meet mine through the clear wall. Then they roll up in the back of her head, leaving only the whites visible. Her face goes slack. She begins to convulse.

I attack the door in a frenzy. This isn't happening. I am not losing my sister today.

My warpknife slices through the locking mechanism and I burst out onto the promenade. Forsaken watch me charge past, nothing more than mild interest on their artificial faces.

In five strides I'm inside the pyramid room. Only Spanner stands between Ianna and me.

I lunge at the Forsaken, launching a flurry of blows. I have to get past him quickly: Ianna needs me now.

I don't see Spanner move. One second I'm moving toward him, and the next I'm hanging in the air, suspended from thick cables around my shoulders and waist. Smaller wires extend out to bind my arms and legs, completing the job. I'm completely helpless.

Spanner's carbon face is cold. "Patience, human. Your sister is not being harmed; the interface is connecting with her brain, that is all."

"That's all?" I croak. Horror ices my spine as I see the thick black cable pushing into the hole they've drilled in Ianna's skull. The cable flexes and pulses like Spanner's quills.

My sister convulses a final time, then falls limp in the chair. A thin line of drool trails from the corner of her mouth.

"What have you done?" I struggle against the cables, but it's hopeless. Suspended off the ground, I have no leverage to fight. I'm as helpless as an exposed shellbaby.

I blink back hot tears, choking on fear and frustration. I never should have let Ianna come out here with us. But was she any better off in the Outsider complex? If I'd left her back there, she'd be dodging bombs right now. Maybe bringing her out to the scablands was a mistake. Maybe she was better off in the Carlyle estate. She might have been a slave, but at least she was safe. If I'd never pulled her out of there, my sister would still be whole, and she wouldn't have cyborg cables burrowing into her brain.

Ianna's back arches, and she makes a horrible choking sound. My heart jumps up into my throat.

Then she sucks in a great gulp of air and settles back into the chair, her chest rising and falling in a steady rhythm. I almost faint with relief. After a moment, her eyes flicker open.

She looks around groggily, then her gaze sharpens as the lighted pyramid captures her attention.

"Ianna," I gasp. Then again, louder. "Ianna!"

She starts and turns. Her eyes look at me without recognition.

"Ianna, it's me. It's Twist. Theo."

"Theo?" My name calls her mind back from whatever frontier has swallowed it. Her eyes sharpen and focus on me. "Theo? What are you doing here?"

"I came to get you out. Those things put a cable in your skull."

She cocks her head at this, considering. Then her eyes light in wonder.

"Yes, I am connected to the Forsaken network now. It's … Oh, Theo. It's incredible. So much life. So much energy. You have no idea…" Her eyes start to lose focus again.

"Ianna!" She starts again, but I can tell I've only got half her attention now. The pull of the network is too strong. I speak fast, struggling to get the words before she drifts off. "Ianna, don't do this. You don't have to do this."

She smiles with half her mouth, her eyes turning back to the pyramid. "You don't understand, Theo. You don't understand at all…"

"Ianna. Ianna!"

But she's gone. Hypnotized by the lights and shapes. Lost inside the network.

Spanner lowers himself into the chair opposite her. As he settles his head onto the headrest, the black cable snakes forward. I shudder as it noses forward like a blind cave crawler, inserting itself into the base of his skull.

All the other chairs around the pyramid are empty. Now it is just Spanner against my sister.

Ianna's face goes still, the familiar line of concentration slashing down between her eyebrows. The colors and shapes accelerate as she focuses in on the puzzle.

I can't breathe. My sister's life balances on the edge, and all I can do is watch.

The colors are reflected in the surface of Spanner's black carbon face. His electric blue eyes flare as he says a single word.

"Begin."

The pyramid flashes once, like a strobe in the dark, so bright I'm left with a red afterimage on the insides of my clamped-shut eyelids. Then the world goes black.

When I open my eyes again, only the outline of the pyramid is visible, a dim ghost in the center of the room. Ianna's face is a pale reflection, her eyes intent yet unfocused. Like a sleepwalker staring into worlds beyond worlds.

A blue shape appears on the pyramid, a polyhedron buried deep inside the projection. Ianna's unfocused gaze touches it for an instant, then changes direction, deft as a flitbat in the dark. An orange shape appears elsewhere in the pyramid.

Blue and orange shapes appear and disappear, filling out the pyramid. For a long time I watch with no understanding of what is happening. Then I notice that wherever their edges touch, a shape will change color, shifting from blue to orange or the reverse. Sometimes when this happens, it creates a cascade effect—wide swaths of the pyramid shifting hue in the blink of an eye. Finally, I think I get it. Ianna has the orange pieces; Spanner has blue. The object of the game is to make all your opponent's pieces shift to match yours.

The crease between Ianna's eyes gets deeper as the game stretches. The pyramid is a seething mass of hundreds of shapes, with virtually no empty space to be claimed. Every new piece placed shifts nearly a quarter of the pyramid to match its color. Spanner's carbon face remains as unreadable as ever, but something in the angle of his body tells me they are entering the endgame. I hang in my nest of wires, tense as a duelist, barely daring to breathe.

Spanner places a piece and half the pyramid becomes blue in a blink. Ianna jerks back in her chair as if slapped. My mouth fills with dust.

Ianna sits motionless for what feels like an hour, the crease between her eyes getting deeper and deeper. I try to study the pyramid, but I can't see the patterns, just an abstract swirl of geometry, like someone's shoved all the constellations in a bag and shaken them up.

My sister's life balances on a warpknife edge. I can't remember the last time I sucked in a breath. I don't even remember what breath is.

Something flickers across Ianna's face. A flutter of expression here and gone again. My heart stutters against my ribs. The expression comes back, and this time I recognize it. I've seen that look a hundred times before.

An orange piece blinks in the pyramid. It's buried so deep that for a moment I think I've imagined it.

Then the cascade begins.

Orange spirals out from the heart of the pyramid, exponential acceleration at every step … and then the whole pyramid is orange, every single corner, all the way to the tips.

I stare at it, my mouth dangling open. Does that really mean what I think it means? The world pauses, caught in the moment between dream and reality.

Then the pyramid goes dark and the only light in the room is the cold blue of Spanner's eyes.

The cyborg's voice grinds up from a deep, dark crevice, so faint I almost don't hear it at all, "Impossible."

Ianna screams. The world lurches back into motion.

I thrash toward my sister, fighting the cables that hold me with desperate strength. The Forsaken has cheated her somehow. She hasn't won at all.

The timbre of her scream finally penetrates my consciousness. She's not screaming in pain or fear. That scream is pure fierce joy.

Relief hits me so hard my knees buckle. If it weren't for the cables holding me up, I'd collapse on the floor right now.

She did it.

My little sister beat the cyborg at his own game.

Abruptly, the cables release me, and I really am lying on the floor. Ianna looks down at me, her eyes shining as bright as Spanner's electric orbs. Her triumphant teeth are so innocent and savage they give me vertigo. She is childlike and ancient. A core of cold cunning sprinkled with guileless purity.

I don't recognize her at all.

Spanner's voice thunders, "Impossible!" Cold metal clamps around me. A bot drags me across the hall by my ankle, as unconcerned with my squalling as a stone cliff. Ianna is shoved back into the cell with me, the door forced shut behind us, the bright arc of a welding torch sealing us off from the outside world once again.

I leap to my feet and pound on the wall, but passing Forsaken take no notice of me. Spanner is nowhere to be found.

Shadow pulls me away. "Leave it, Twist."

"Leave it?" I round on her in disbelief. "Ianna beat that spine-sucker fair and square and you want me to leave it?"

"We've got more important things to worry about right now. I just saw Ghengis and Rory headed toward the council chamber."

26

I go cold with shock. Ghengis is the sadistic giant who tormented me during our training in Merrimac. Rory's the spine-sucker who double-crossed our crew during the final exam. They're both governor Julius's lapdogs now, and they helped thwart our attempt to assassinate Julius when we thought taking him out would stop the Guardian's big attack on the Outsiders.

"What are they doing here?" I croak. Ghengis and Rory are the last people I'd expect to see out here in the wastes.

"Hunting us, would be my guess." Shadow peers through the transparent wall cautiously.

"How do they even know we're out here?"

"The checkpoint," Rust says. "Someone must have ID'd us when we broke through the Guardian's lines."

I'm pacing now, the little cell suddenly cramped and crowded around me. "Would the Forsaken hand us over to the Guardians?"

Shadow shakes her head.

"It's hard to say. Most of them didn't seem interested in getting involved in human affairs. But we don't know what Ghengis is offering them, either. Maybe they need some resource Canyon City can provide."

"Spines." I pound the wall with my fist. "How many Guardians did they have with them?"

"I don't know. I saw four, but odds are they've got more waiting outside."

"We need to get out of this box. Now."

"I'm on it." Shadow squats and starts working at the welded seam with her warpknife.

"Then what?" Ianna asks. "We don't know how to get out of here. We don't even know where the Beast is."

"That way," Knott points down the hall. "The Beast is that way."

"How do you know that?"

She grins and pulls a little tracker from her pocket.

I grin in return. "Brilliant. So we go that way."

"What about getting help?" Ianna says. "I just beat Spanner at that spine-sucking pyramid game. Doesn't he have to help us now?"

"It doesn't look like Spanner's going to keep his word," I growl. "And we won't be able to help anyone if Ghengis and Rory get their hands on us. The first step is getting our freedom back."

"Got it." Shadow pushes the door open. "Let's go."

Knott and I take the lead. Rust brings up the rear. The promenade hums with hidden machinery, but it's suddenly deserted.

"Where did all the Forsaken go?" Shadow asks.

"I don't know," I say. "Sunbathing?"

She shoots me an acid look, which I think is unfair. I wasn't entirely kidding. If they get energy from the sun, maybe they really are sunbathing.

I squint as we step out into a bright afternoon. The streets are as empty as the inside.

Shadow has a point. The lack of Forsaken right now is really weird.

Knott leads us into what looks like a junkyard. Old machinery and spare parts are piled in neat, four-meter stacks, making the whole place a labyrinth.

"It's like a metal scablands." I run my finger along a stack. It comes away brown with rust.

"Hopefully with fewer Horrors," Shadow says. "Let's spread out so we can watch each other's flanks. You go one row to the left, and I'll go one to the right."

I creep forward through rusting metal and sun-bleached carbon. The silence is getting to me. I mean, I like silence. But that's underground, where it's supposed to be silent. This place feels like it should be bustling with people.

Cannon fire shatters the quiet.

"Guardians!" Shadow shouts. "Run!"

Another shot sears past me, burning a stack of old gears beside my helmet. I pound forward, my breath loud in my ears. I try to shift my focus to my blind eye, using my greicagin-sight to get a fix on our attackers, but their steady cannon fire keeps me ducking and weaving, making it impossible to concentrate.

"Jmini, launch a mapping drone."

A hatch slides open above my shoulder blade, launching the little sphere skyward. "Aye aye, Capitan."

I return fire as I run, turning at random in the maze, trying to lose them in the stacks. I round a corner—and skid to a halt.

"Kass?"

A Forsaken city in the middle of the wastes is pretty much the last place you expect to run into your ex-girlfriend.

"Twist." Kass looks less shocked than I am. She's got a cannon leveled at my chest. "There you are."

"Were you looking for me?" I stammer in confusion.

Something tightens inside my chest. Kass looks good. Blue eyes flashing over red-gold skin. Soft lips over perfect teeth.

"No, I'm taking a sightseeing tour of the wastes. Of course I've been looking for you. And now I've found you."

"But why?"

Her eyes go cold.

"Why? You're a traitor to Canyon City. How do you think that makes me look, Twist? Do you know how many times I've been questioned since you defected? I spent a week in a cell while they decided what to do with me. The only way for me to prove I'm not collaborating with you is to bring your head in on a spike."

I think about the message I've written to her, stored in Jmini's memory. The message telling her how I feel and explaining everything. Apologizing.

She doesn't look like someone who wants to hear my apologies right now.

"Well that's graphic. You wouldn't really put my head on a spike, would you?"

"It's a figure of speech, Twist. But don't tempt me." She frowns. "What happened to your eye?"

My hand jerks reflexively toward my blind eye. The eye that gives me my greicagin sight. The last time I saw Kass was before Julius took my eye. Before he took my dad.

"Julius." I spit the name through my teeth.

Her expression softens. "An eye for an eye, huh? How biblical of him."

A pair of Guardians step up and flank her. I don't like these odds.

"Put your hands up. I don't want to hurt you, Twist. But I will if I have to."

I raise my hands, checking the map in the corner of my display. According to Jmini's drone, the others are still moving, getting farther away with every passing second. They've got at least a half-dozen Guardians on their tail. No help there.

"Kass, it doesn't have to be this way. I knew it would look bad when they figured out I was working with the Outsiders. I knew suspicion would fall on you. I pushed you away because I was trying to protect you. I didn't want my choices to affect your career."

"My career? This is bigger than my career. What about my life, Twist? Even my friends look at me funny. No matter how many interrogations I pass, they still can't believe I wasn't working with you. You ruined my life." Kass's face is flushed with anger. "Put the cuffs on him."

The two Guardians keep their cannons trained on me as they approach. If I'm going to make a break for it, I'm running out of time.

I check the map again. It's still just the four of us, but more Guardian blips are on the way. I shift my attention to my blind eye and find my sight.

The Guardians glow with energy. I watch it shift within them as they approach, flaring in each limb a fraction of a second before it moves.

My breath catches as I consider what I'm about to attempt. Rust is the only person whose movements I've ever tried to anticipate, and that was in training. If I fail now, I'll end up dead.

"Ready the message dart in the drone," I subvocalize to Jmini. "I'm not going down without at least explaining myself to Kass. She deserves that much."

The Guardian to my left lowers his cannon and starts to reach for the manacles.

"Now!"

Jmini's drone fires the message dart at Kass, along with a couple of tiny snapdragon missiles as a distraction.

I drop my shoulder and dive toward the Guardian still covering me. The energy in his trigger finger flares. As I reach for my warpknife, I twist my torso so the cannon blast glances off my chestplate. The wind huffs out of me. At such close range, even a glancing blow feels like being kicked by a Hubzoh. I grit my teeth and continue my movement, swinging my warpknife up across the barrel, shearing the cannon cleanly in two.

Then I'm behind him, rolling across the ground. His partner has his hands back on his cannon, his finger tightening. He's got a clean shot at my exposed back. In desperation, I reach for the energy in his hand and yank.

The shot goes wide.

27

Sometimes I feel like all I do is run. I ran after Mink in the mines. I ran from the Horror to get to the final qualifier. I ran after Kass during our final exam, and Jepet in the caves.

And here I am, running again. Stick to what you're good at, I guess.

I pound between the stacks of parts, dodging cannon fire. The Guardians behind me are not amused at my escape. Kass is probably livid.

At least I got to deliver my message. She may never forgive me, but at least she'll hear what I have to say. That's something, right?

A cannon blast punches me in the back of the shoulder and I stumble, nearly sprawling on my face.

Right. More running, less thinking.

My display shows three Guardians behind me and six ahead. My crew is beyond that. I've always been fast, but I'll need every scrap of speed and luck to survive this.

There is good news though. My crew has reached the Beast. Knott's up in the turret, keeping the Guardians at bay. Getting through the line of Guardians to join my crew is going to be the tricky part.

Another shot sizzles past my ear. I flinch away and almost decapitate myself on the protruding end of a rusty I-beam. Spines. It's really hard trying to look ahead and make plans while people are shooting at you.

Knott's gun has forced the Guardians to spread out in an arc and take cover. Unfortunately, that arc is directly between the Beast and where I am. I open a channel to the crew.

"Knott, can you hear me?"

For a second all I hear is the steady whump of her turret cannon. Then her voice comes faint over the line.

"I read you, Twist. Where are you?"

"I'm coming in fast at six o'clock. I need you to cover me as I break through the Guardians' lines."

"You got it."

There's ten meters of open ground between the Beast and the Guardians' cover. Ten meters of Guardians shooting at my exposed back. This is not going to be fun.

"I see you, Twist," Shadow breaks in. "Relax, we've all got you covered."

"Relax?" I bark in disbelief. "Sure, whatever you say, Shadow. Jelly easy."

The entire crew opens fire as I break cover, forcing the Guardians to duck away. At least, that's the plan.

In reality, Knott has the only gun powerful enough to do any damage to the Guardians' armor. So the ducking is entirely optional on their part. And judging by the shots sizzling around me, at least a few of them have declined that option.

I'm only three meters into the clear space when a shot hits the back of my knee, punching my leg out from under me.

I sprawl on my face, but manage to turn it into a roll. As I get back to my feet, another shot hits me in the ribs. Two more steps and two more shots burn into my back. That's four shots in four meters. Spines, I'm not going to make it.

Then something explodes into the Guardians behind me. I hear screams of surprise and pain.

The cannons stop hitting me, and I stumble the rest of the way to the Beast. Rust gives me a hand up into the cab.

"Thanks," I gasp. "What's happening?"

"It looks like we've got a friend."

I follow his gaze out the windshield.

A black tornado is churning through the Guardians. Three of them are down, and the others have their warpknives out, defending desperately.

The Forsaken fights like nothing I've ever seen before. He's like a dust-devil, his body launching attacks from every direction simultaneously. Missiles blast from his back. Cannons pulse from his legs. Spikes shoot from his fingers.

Spanner has come to our aid.

The first thing I feel is stunned relief. The second is triumph.

Then I remember that Kass is out there. She doesn't stand a chance against that thing.

I search the remaining Guardians with my sight. There. She's crouched down, using one of the stacks as cover. Spanner is five meters away, engaged with a trio of Guardians.

I watch one of them fall. Then another.

Any second, Spanner's going to finish off the last one. Then he'll turn his attention to Kass.

I do the only thing I can think of. I release a flight of snapdragon missiles.

They strike the stack above Kass in a burst of smoke and sound. For a heartbeat, the stack teeters and sways. Then the whole thing comes crashing down, burying Kass beneath a mound of rubble.

I wince. That definitely hurt.

"Sorry, Kass."

Her armor will protect her from the worst of it. She'll be able to walk away, once she digs herself out. I hope.

It's still a better chance than she would have had against Spanner.

The Forsaken stalks over to the Beast.

"Go south. We will catch up with you."

I gape at him. "You're going to help us?"

I try to imagine what an entire army of Forsaken could do. I picture them tearing through the ranks of the Guardians, an unstoppable cyborg whirlwind.

For the first time, I believe we might have a chance to win this war.

Spanner ignores me, turning his blue eyes to Ianna.

"You have earned my respect. I will help you, and I will bring a few others who do not bury their heads in the sand."

Oh. Not an army, then.

Still, judging by what Spanner did to those Guardians, even a few Forsaken could make a world of difference.

"Thank you," I say. "We'll meet you to the south."

The Beast thrums to life. With a clatter and crunching of gears, we roar back out into the wasteland.

28

———

On the way out of the Forsaken city, I can't stop thinking about Kass. I feel bad for pushing her away. I'm sorry I abandoned her in Canyon City and left her to take all the heat for me defecting to the Outsiders. I feel guilty for dropping a ton scrap metal on her head.

Most of all, I regret that I never told Kass the truth about my dad, and Ianna, and the Outsiders. And about how much she meant to me. How much she means to me still.

At least I got my message to her. I know it's too little, too late—but it's better than nothing. Maybe she'll hate me less after she reads it.

Though she may hate me more for dropping that stack of metal on her head.

"She'll be fine, Twist." Jmini pipes up, as if reading my thoughts. "Her armor protected her from the scraps. She'll dig herself out and be back to hunting you in no time."

I snort.

"I find that both reassuring and terrifying."

"Then my work here is done."

We're nearing the outskirts of the city. Empty streets roll by through the Beast's armored windows.

"I guess cyborgs don't get outside much," I say.

"It's not the cyborgs I'm worried about. Ghengis and Rory are still out there." Shadow's got that faraway look in her eye that means she's focused on her retina display. Probably looking at a real-time map.

"Hopefully they're still meeting with the Forsaken council. Do you think there are more Guardians watching the perimeter of the city?"

"I don't know. We escaped almost a dozen of them back there. If we're lucky, that's all they brought."

"I wouldn't count on it." Rust leans forward in the back seat. "At the very least, they would have left a few behind to guard their vehicles."

"Spines, Theo. How bad do they want you back?" Ianna asks.

"Maybe it's not me Julius wants," I retort.

Ianna shrinks in her seat, her face going pale. I regret my words immediately.

"Sorry. That was a bad joke."

"Not funny." She wraps her arms around herself and starts to hum low under her breath. Self-comforting. She did that when she was a little girl too.

"Nothing about this is funny," Shadow agrees. "Twist's psycho ex-girlfriend is chasing him all over the wastes, and she's got Ghengis, Rory, and a squad of Guardians with her. I think this qualifies as a bad day."

"She's not psycho," I snap. "She has good reason to be angry. You'd be angry too if your girlfriend defected to the other side and left all of your friends wondering if you were a traitor. And we did get some help. We just don't know how much yet."

Shadow peers out the window. "Judging by how empty this city is, I wouldn't get your hopes up. Even if all of the Forsaken came back with us, would they be enough to make a dent in the Guardians?"

"That one back there made a dent," Knott chimes in from her turret.

Rust nods. "Knott raises a good point. Sheer numbers may not be the correct way to measure the Forsaken's impact."

"I'll give you that," Shadow says. "But that doesn't change the fact that there are thousands of Guardians. Even if every Forsaken is worth a dozen of them, which I doubt, but let's say they are for the sake of argument, we'd still need hundreds of Forsaken fighting on our side to even the odds."

My mind drifts as they argue. I think about what Rust said before, about us not going about this the right way. How we're fighting the Guardians on their chosen battlefield, not ours.

How can we change that? And more importantly, what kind of battlefield would suit us better?

I turn the problem over in my mind, but the answer eludes me. I feel like the solution is right there, obvious if I could only see it. I grind my teeth in frustration.

The Forsaken city ends as if we're stepping off a cliff. One minute we're rolling through the outskirts, and the next there's nothing but flat desert in every direction.

"It's like we're on another planet," Ianna says in a soft voice.

"Or stepping off one," I amend. "Being in that city was like being on one of Greica's moons."

"Interplanetary travel without leaving the comfort of your own Beast." Shadow grins. "We may be onto something here. Think of the demand."

I shake my head. "I think there would be less demand than you think. Neither of our destinations are particularly desirable for the upwardly mobile traveler."

"Oh, I don't know," Rust chimes in. "Any destination can be made to look desirable. It's all in the marketing. You just need the right slogan. 'Get away from it all in the wasteland.'"

"Wander the wasteland," Shadow says.

"Get lost in the wasteland," Ianna tries.

Jmini's voice crackles over the cab speaker.

"April is the cruelest month, breeding

Lilacs out of the dead land, mixing

Memory and desire, stirring

Dull roots with spring rain."

Four sets of eyes turn to me. I throw up my hands.

"Don't look at me. I don't know what he's rambling on about."

"It's 'The Waste Land' by T.S. Eliot, you uncultured philistines," Jmini huffs.

Rust's hoarse voice creaks with laughter. "Your AI recites poetry? That's a first."

"We've all got our quirks, Mr. Rides-a-Rock-Horror," Jmini shoots back.

"Touché."

"Where is Akona, anyway?" I ask.

"She's safe."

"Will we see her again?"

"She'll be back when the time is right." Rust smiles enigmatically.

"I hate to break up the party, but we've got incoming." Shadow's voice is sharp.

I groan.

"Again? Haven't we dodged enough cannon fire for one day?"

"I'm not sure what's in it yet, but we've got a dust cloud coming up fast on our tail."

I unsling my cannon and climb into the back. Knott swings her turret around to the rear. The dust cloud is a speck on the horizon, but it's mushrooming quickly. Whoever it is, they're closing fast.

"It's the Forsaken," Shadow yells.

"Friend or foe?" I ask.

"I don't know, they're not talking."

"Wonderful. Why can't things be easy for a change? Is that too much to ask?"

My stomach twists as the cloud grows closer. The last time we tried to run from the Forsaken, they captured us as easily as if we were children. And this time I don't even have a gravbike to run on. What if they're coming to take us back to the Guardians? What if they're coming to kill us?

"Whose dumb idea was it to come to the Forsaken for help again?" I mutter. "We should have stayed in Canyon City and fought the Guardians ourselves."

The Forsaken's vehicles are visible in the dust now. Blocky black metal stretching in strange directions. I remember their net slamming me to the ground. My gravbike twisted around me like wire.

I grip my cannon with sweat-slick hands.
They're five hundred meters out.
Four hundred.
Three.
The com crackles to life.
"This is Spanner. We are here to fight."

29

———

Our camp sprawls across the floor of the canyon. The low morning sun pushes long shadows across the sand and white frost coats the metal shells of the vehicles. The monsoons are over. Winter has truly arrived.

My breath steams in the frigid air as I cup my hands around a mug of matté, soaking in the warmth. Rust stands with me. We've just finished a pre-dawn sparring session, and I'm sweaty and exhausted. By contrast, the ancient legend looks like he could go another ten rounds. I don't know how he does it.

A dozen Forsaken vehicles are scattered about, blocky, asymmetrical shapes against the smooth, curving landscape. Each one carries a handful of Forsaken. According to Spanner, there are less than a hundred of them.

"It's not enough," I say quietly.

"No," Rust agrees. "It's not."

I watch the Forsaken scuttle around the camp, doing incomprehensible things. At times they'll stop and stare into space for long stretches of time. I see what Jmini meant about them not being human anymore. The more you watch them, the more you realize they've become an alien species. Trying to understand them is like trying to understand a hive of plakbeetles.

"Do you think we can trust them?" I ask.

Rust shrugs.

"Your sister seems to think we can."

I follow his gaze and find Ianna sitting in a camp chair across from Spanner. There's a delicate pyramid of wire suspended in the air between them, forming the playing field for the puzzle game.

It still looks like a jumbled mess to me, but Ianna's pattern-loving mind is drawn to the game like a flitbat to light. The Forsaken seem almost as fascinated by her as they are the game. They've never met a human who could even understand the game, let alone challenge them at it.

Ianna's stayed near Spanner in the days since the Forsaken joined us. The whole thing makes me uncomfortable, especially the wires she plugs into her skull, but she's engaged and less angry than she's been since we pulled her out of the Carlyle estate. I suppose to her the Forsaken are an interesting problem to solve.

I sigh and tilt my head back, looking up at two stubborn stars lingering defiantly in the face of the rising sun. We haven't been able to get in touch with Tempest, or any of the Outsider bases. Our only indication they're still alive is the low rumble of Guardian bombs in the distance. We're camped about five kilometers outside their perimeter. From here on, things are going to get hairy.

I sigh. "I wish we could fly away. Find another world to colonize. Leave the IEC and the Guardians and all this madness behind."

"If wishes were fishes, no one would starve," Rust says.

"What the dust does that mean?"

"It's something my mother used to say when I was a kid. It means there's no point wasting your time wishing. You have to work with what you have."

"What we have is a hundred Forsaken and whatever is left of the Outsiders." I sip my matté, savoring the liquid warmth inside my chest. "It doesn't look good."

"No it doesn't. At least your friends from the Forsaken city never caught up to us."

I sweep my eyes over the horizon nervously.

"Not yet they haven't. I'm sure they'll be back. Rory and Kass aren't going to let me off that easily, and Ghengis will seize any opportunity to kill someone."

"Heav'n hath no Rage, like Love to Hatred turn'd,

Nor Hell a Fury, like a Woman scorn'd," Jmini says.

"Sure, but what's Rory's excuse?" I ask.

"An eye for an eye and a tooth for a tooth?"

"I've only got one eye left, Jmini. I'd like to hold on to it."

"Perhaps a hand for a hand then."

"If I give Rory my hand, do you think he'll stop hunting me?"

"I doubt it. Perhaps he's simply a spiny pill."

"There's no 'perhaps' about it."

"We could replace that eye, if you wish." Spanner crunches up to our table, Ianna right behind him.

I scratch the skin beside my shrunken white orb self-consciously. "No, thank you. I don't have time for major surgery right now."

"The time involved would be less than an hour. The eye would be operational immediately."

Spanner's electric blue eyes burn like miniature stars. I wonder if they function like my retina screen? I'd bet good credits there's a lot more to them than that.

The bigger question is, would a mechanical eye affect my greicagin-sight? That talent has become focused through my blind eye. If I replaced the eye, would I lose the sight? I'd rather not find out.

"No, thank you," I repeat.

Spanner's porcupine-quill heat sinks bristle; he's still prickly with everyone but Ianna. Fortunately, she holds up her hand.

"Humans are illogical," she says. "You have to let them make their own choices."

To my surprise, the Forsaken quiets at her words. I cock an eyebrow at my sister.

"They can't stand to see something operating at less than optimal capacity," she explains. "It's why they've transformed themselves the way they have. They're tinkerers, always striving to make things better."

"Is that why their vehicles look the way they do?"

Ianna smiles and my heart swells. She almost looks happy for the first time since we rescued her.

"Yes, that's exactly it. They're constantly adding things and improving them."

"And this makes sense to you?"

"It does. It's the first thing that's made sense in a long time."

Looking into Ianna's eyes, I'm struck by the sharp intelligence in them. They're no longer the eyes of a child. It hits me that my little sister is all grown up.

"All right. Good. I'm happy for you."

"You should at least wear an eye patch," Shadow says from right behind me.

I jump, sloshing matté over my hand.

"Warn a guy next time." I shake hot liquid from my fingers.

Shadow smiles. Her face is puffy and there's a pillow-crease down her cheek.

"What would be the fun in that? But honestly, that shriveled eye is gross. I made you this." She holds out a black eyepatch.

I eye it warily.

"Isn't that a bit cliche?"

Shadow shrugs.

"If you're not going to get the eye replaced, and you're not wearing your bandages anymore, what other option is there? Besides, it's not as cliche as you think." She tosses it to me.

The patch isn't soft, like I expected. Instead, it's a black carbon disc, padded on the underside. It rings when I tap it with my fingertip.

I raise an eyebrow at Shadow. "What's it made of?"

"Armor plating," she smirks. "And it's got a small, localized grav-field built in that will keep it stuck to your face. No strap necessary."

"Impressive. You did this all yourself?"

"No, Knott helped with the fabrication, and Ianna helped with the gravfield tech."

Knott blushes behind the cook pot, while Ianna beams.

"Wait, you and Ianna worked together? Voluntarily?" My shocked gaze goes from Shadow to Ianna and back again.

Shadow grins. "She's been growing on me. Ever since the Forsaken joined us she's a lot easier to deal with."

Ianna narrows her eyes at that, then huffs good-naturedly. "I guess I can't argue with that. I have been feeling a lot better lately."

I marvel at the two of them. Wonders never cease.

"Thank you. Both of you. All of you." I place the carbon disc over my eye, and it sticks to the socket with a soft feeling of suction. The padding makes it surprisingly comfortable. "How do I look?"

"Arrrr, Capitan," Jmini growls. "Now we be ready for battle."

30

Knott ladles out bowls of hot porridge while Shadow calls up a 3-D map of the area.

"I think we need to hit them where they aren't," Shadow says. "Get the Guardians to pull back."

"Where would that be?" I ask.

"I agree," Rust says. "We should hit them inside the wall. Make them pull the Guardians back from the scablands. Give the Outsiders a chance to regroup."

I stare into the sunrise, thinking it over.

"How would we do that? And where would we hit them? We already tried to hit the Mesa once, and we all know how that turned out."

"Not the Mesa," Shadow says. "Some place important, though. Something they'll care enough to protect."

"And what's that?"

"What do the IEC care about more than anything?" Rust asks.

"Greicagins," I say immediately. Then it hits me. "The transport yard."

The wrinkles on Rust's face deepen as he grins.

"Yes, the transport yard. Every greicagin that comes out of the mines goes through the transport yard. If we hit that, the Guardians will scurry home like rats."

"But how do we get past the wall?"

"The slave tunnels," Shadow says.

My mouth curls in a wicked grin.

"That's brilliant. Imagine Jepet's face when we come storming up through his cellar."

Shadow returns my smile. "He deserves everything that's coming to him."

"Yes. Yes, he does. Rust, do you remember that cavern where I first encountered Akona? Can you get us back to that?"

The old warrior nods.

"I can. But it will be difficult to get there. The Guardians control that part of the scablands."

I sigh. "Of course they do. Is it too much to ask for something to be easy? Just once?"

Shadow smiles tiredly and rubs her eyes. "What would be the fun of that?" She highlights a section of the map in red. "We're going to have to get across ten kilometers of occupied land. The Guardians are spread pretty thin on the ground, but we'll still have to watch out for patrols."

"We'll be moving a large force," Rust points out. "It's safe to assume they'll notice us at some point."

"Hopefully that point won't be until we're close to the objective," I say.

"Why do we not create a distraction?" Spanner asks. "Are they not more likely to overlook us if their attention is drawn elsewhere?"

I shake my head. "In case you haven't noticed, there's not that many of us. We can't afford to waste any of our people on a suicide run."

"Who said anything about suicide?" Spanner pins me with his electric blue eyes. "A few of my people could draw the necessary attention without risk."

I think about the way Spanner cut through Kass's people back in the Forsaken city. A handful of similar whirlwinds could draw a lot of attention. I nod thoughtfully.

"Ok. They're your people, so we'll trust your judgment on this. Now we need to figure out how best to deploy them."

Shadow highlights a route across the map.

"This is probably our best path. We'll have to go slow so I can scout ahead as we move."

"Drones?" I ask.

"No, they'll pick up the power signature of any drones. I'll have to do it on foot."

I frown down at the map. "I don't like it. You're too valuable to risk."

"We can be of assistance here as well," Spanner says.

"You have scouts?" I ask.

"Yes."

Shadow crinkles her nose. "Are they any good?"

"Yes."

The Forsaken leader and Shadow lock eyes for a long moment. Finally, she nods. "OK."

Shouts rise in the Forsaken part of camp. Alarms and whistles sound. I'm on my feet in an instant, warpknife humming in my hand.

Spanner doesn't hesitate; he's up and moving before most of us have even realized something's happening. All I can do is pound along in his wake.

As I round one of the blocky vehicles, the problem comes into focus. Standing on the edge of the camp, towering over half a dozen Forsaken warriors, are three Rock Horrors. Blue and white streaks ripple along the lead creature's carapace as it crouches down on all six legs, crystalline pincers raised, ready to pounce.

My gut twists as I realize it's not just any Rock Horror. It's Akona.

"Stop!" I scream, sprinting to get between them.

But I'm too slow, and the distance across the camp is too great. One of the Forsaken darts in, attacking in a blur. Akona reacts quickly, but not quickly enough. The Forsaken swings a sparking rod at her forward leg, two blows connecting in quick succession. Blue-white lightning flares at the impact.

Akona shrieks and lashes out with her pincer, the force of the blow sending the Forsaken warrior tumbling over and over in the dust.

A second Forsaken lunges at one of the other Hubzoh. More lightning flashes.

This one isn't as fortunate as his comrade. The Hubzoh catches the warrior's arm in a massive pincer, snipping it off at the elbow in one clean cut. The Forsaken goes down, trailing bright sparks.

"Stop!" I scream again, as I finally arrive at the scene. I thrust myself between the two sides, arms extended.

All eyes are on me now, both the electric blue variety and the big, multi-faceted kind. None of them seem very happy to see me. I try to swallow, my mouth going dry.

"Stop," I repeat. "We're on the same side."

Spanner stalks up to me, all his quills standing on end. His blue eyes crackle, boring into mine.

"Step aside, human."

"This is Akona. She's a friend."

"A friend? This monster is an abomination. Step aside or I will cut you down where you stand."

An image of Spanner annihilating Kass's squad flashes through my head, sending a chill down my spine. If the Forsaken leader elects to go through me, I won't stand a chance.

Still, I lift my chin defiantly.

"They aren't monsters. The Hubzoh are intelligent creatures. This is their home. We're the invaders here."

Spanner's black carbon face remains stoic—but I can feel electricity crackling through the air, making my hair stand on end. Sweat slicks my palms, while some ancient danger alarm in the back of my mind is screaming. I feel like I'm standing under an overhang, with the whole cliff face about to tumble down onto my head.

Then Rust arrives, his ancient armored shoulder slotting in next to mine.

"This creature saved my life." His voice is quiet and firm, and his words carry easily in the charged silence. "I will not let you hurt her."

Shadow skids into line next, followed by Knott. Their faces are grim.

Spanner runs his eyes over the four of us, then glares up at Akona.

For a moment, I think he's going to cut his way through all of us. Then he snarls and turns away.

"Have it your way, humans. We will not kill these Horrors. For now."

My head spins, the adrenaline draining out of me so abruptly I almost fall.

Knott catches my shoulder. "Are you all right?"

"Yeah, just dandy. We should start every day like this."

Behind me, Rust and Akona are enjoying their reunion, the old soldier running his hands over Akona's carapace. Trails of golden light follow his fingertips.

The Hubzoh catches my eye, and I feel amusement from her.

"Sure, you can laugh about it," I tell her. "Me, I'm going to have to change my pants."

I stagger off to do just that.

31

The Hubzoh turn out to be emissaries of a sort. Akona has brought friends. Communication is difficult, but from what we can tell, it sounds like she's been off spreading the word among her kind that not all humans want to kill them. The two Hubzoh she's brought back with her are the first to join our cause. With any luck, they'll be the first of many.

Between the Hubzoh and the Forsaken, we've now picked up two strong allies in a number of days. Our insurgency is small but growing. A spark of hope flickers within me.

Of course, the fact that the two groups hate each other complicates things. Two more fights almost break out between them on the first day. After that, we put the Hubzoh in a cave far from the Forsaken camp, just to be safe. When we all pack up and move out, we let the Forsaken scout far out front with Shadow, while Rust keeps the Hubzoh back as our rear guard. It's a clunky solution, but it's the best we can do for now.

Halfway across the occupied zone, Shadow picks up a distress call from an Outsider base. She sends a pair of Forsaken scouts to check it out, in case it's a Guardian trap.

She needn't have bothered. The Outsider base is cold and silent as I step in out of the afternoon glare.

The smell hits me first, like meat rotting in a sewer, making me pull my scarf up over my mouth and nose.

It looks like the Outsiders made their last stand in the dining hall. Bodies are strewn across the cavern, hundreds of them. It doesn't seem real. Surely this kind of slaughter only exists in vids.

I come upon a woman who has been charred and vivisected, her torso peeled open, internal organs spilling into pools of darkening blood.

I lose what remains of my breakfast.

Shadow hands me a towel when I'm done. Her eyes are brimming with tears.

I wipe my burning mouth and spit. When I try to speak, my voice shakes.

"How could they do this? They killed everyone. Men, women, children..."

She shakes her head.

"I don't know. I keep thinking that could have been us."

"Being alive doesn't make me feel better right now."

"No, I mean we could have been the killers. This was done by Guardians, Twist. People we ate dinner with at Merrimac. Sat next to in class."

"They were just following orders." I blurt the thing they always say. The thing that supposedly justifies any action.

But staring at the bodies around me, the words sound hollow in my ears. As if they're an IEC official statement. Like I'm listening to someone else saying them.

"That's not an excuse," she insists. "No orders could ever make me kill children in their home. This is wrong. This is evil."

"That's why we're fighting them, isn't it? To prevent things like this from happening?"

"It's not enough. People need to know about this."

"What do you mean?"

"I mean, the people of Canyon City still look up to the Guardians. They still think they're being protected." She grabs me by the arm, her dark eyes intense. "We have to tell them the truth. We have to show them this."

"How?"

"We've got to hack into the city's network. Blast it out past the censors. Get it out where everyone can see."

I take a breath and push my hand back through my hair.

"Can you do that?"

"No, but I know someone who can."

It takes me a beat, but then I understand. "You mean Grab."

She nods.

"He's tunneled into every node in the city. If we get him this footage, he'll make sure everyone sees it."

"She's right, Twist." Rust steps up beside me. "The people need to see this. And we need them on our side."

"On our side? What does that have to do with anything?"

"We can't win this fight alone; we're outnumbered too badly. Our first goal is to stop the Guardian assault on the Outsiders. But if we want to do more than that, we'll need the support of the people of Canyon City."

I gape at him. "You want to turn all of the people of Canyon City into Outsiders?"

"No, you're missing the point. The IEC needs the people of Canyon City. Keeping them working is the entire reason the Guardians exist. If they lose the people, they lose the colony."

"Also," Shadow adds with a grim smile, "every Guardian they have to use to keep the people under control is one less Guardian that's trying to kill us. Rust is right. We need the people with us."

Looking at all the bodies around us, I shudder. I can't believe Guardians did this. People I know slaughtered everyone here. I remember what Rust said days ago, about how we're fighting on the wrong battlefield. Letting the Guardians set the rules of engagement. Maybe this is a battlefield we can choose. The battlefield of public opinion. Shadow and Rust are right. The people of Canyon City need to know the truth.

"OK. Get the word out. Do you know how to get in touch with Grab?"

Shadow nods. "He gave me an emergency contact node. As soon as we get this massacre documented, I'll send a drone up and beam him a message."

"Great. Get to it."

I turn to go, but Rust puts a hand on my arm. "No, you need to talk to them."

"Talk to who?"

"The people of Canyon City. It's not enough to show them what's happened here. If we want them on our side, one of us has to speak to them directly. They need a face they can relate to. Someone they'll trust."

I try to pull away. "Why would they trust me?"

"Because you used to be one of them. Then you were a Guardian. And now you're an Outsider. You've stood on every side of this conflict; they can relate to you. No one is in a better position to win the people over than you."

"What about Shadow? Or Knott?"

"No, Rust is right," Shadow says. "You've got more personal stakes, Twist. They killed your dad and kidnapped your sister. You should talk to them. Besides, you like to give speeches." Her mouth quirks mischievously.

I look from Shadow to Rust, but find no escape in their eyes. I throw up my hands.

"Fine. What do I say?"

"Just the truth," Rust says. "Tell the people the truth."

Shadow frames me so the blasted cavern will be in the background, the scattered bodies indistinct but clearly there.

I swallow. My stomach churns as I think about all those people watching me. Judging me. Sweat coats the back of my neck.

"Just be yourself, Twist." Shadow steadies the camera on a flat rock.

"Easy for you to say. Your face isn't going to be streaming into every home in Canyon City."

"Don't think about that," Rust says. "You can't talk to everyone at once. The secret is to talk to one person. Pretend the camera is someone you like."

"Ha-ha."

"He's right, Twist." Shadow catches my gaze, her improbably old eyes holding mine. "Just look at me. Talk to me. You can do this."

I take a deep breath and nod. OK. I can do this. I look into the camera and pretend it's Shadow's eyes.

"People of Canyon City. My name is Twist. I was born a rockhead, just like you."

Once I start talking, the words start to flow. Like they've been all blocked up inside me, just waiting to be let out. I tell them about how Mom died and Dad disappeared. How it was just me and my sister until they took Ianna away from me. The way I searched for years, but couldn't find her.

I tell them about the Guardian Tournament, and Merrimac. The way the game was rigged against us rockheads, but we managed to win anyway.

Emotion roughens my voice as I recount finding my dad alive and living with the Outsiders. I describe the way the Outsiders have to hide underground like animals, hunted and afraid.

I talk about my time as a Guardian, and how I finally tracked down my sister. Anger colors my words as I recall how Ianna was kept as a slave on the Carlyle estate.

Tears run down my cheeks when my story reaches my dad's death. With a cracking voice I tell them of the hundreds of Outsiders who have been killed during the Guardian's assault.

Next, I unveil the way the IEC's campaign of death extends beyond humans, to the native intelligent species of Greica, the Hubzoh. How their scientific team covered everything up and named them Horrors, just so the IEC could mine and export greicagins.

Finally, I show them the carnage around me. The camera pans over the men and women hacked to pieces. Children and grandmothers disemboweled.

Here, I stumble and fall silent for a moment, appalled again at the slaughter. The sheer brutality of the killing.

"I'm not sure what I can say about what we've found here. Words can't capture the extent of this atrocity. Words can't bring these dead people back to life. I guess if I were going to say anything, I'd say that these people fought to live their lives the way they wanted. They fought to be free of the IEC. Free of generations of indentured servitude. Of debt that can never be repaid. Of slavery.

"I don't know why the IEC couldn't leave these people in peace, couldn't let them live their own lives. They weren't hurting anyone: They just wanted to live in peace and freedom. And for that they were slaughtered in their home like vermin."

I have to stop and swallow the lump in my throat.

"Maybe they're in a better place now. Maybe they're just dead. At least they don't have to be afraid anymore." I turn and stare directly into the camera, speaking to every single person watching. I'm no longer scared to talk to them. All of Canyon City needs to hear this. "We're done running. There will be no more hiding, no more living in fear. We are going to fight back and bring down the people responsible for this.

"For three generations we've worked to line the IEC's pockets. Three generations have lived and died in the crimson dust.

"No more.

"Now is the time to fight. To free every single person in Canyon City.

"Join us and we will make sure these people did not die for nothing."

Shadow goes off to transmit the message and I go looking for Knott. I find her slumped in the dust of the cavern, stroking the hair of a dead child. Her face is a map of tear tracks.

"Knott, I've got a job for you."

The big Tank is surprised by the sound of her name. She looks around, dazed, not sure where she is. Finally, her anguished eyes find me, and slowly come back into focus.

I help her to her feet.

"Gather all the explosives you can spare. We're going to bring this cavern down."

"Down?" she echoes, confused.

"We don't have time to bury all of these bodies, and I'm not going to leave them like this. So we'll bring the roof down, and bury them all at once."

Understanding presses her lips into a line.

"Yes. That is good."

A couple of hours later, we all gather outside the base. It's late afternoon, and the sun radiating off the canyon walls holds off the worst of the winter chill.

Everyone seems to be looking at me to say something, but I'm all talked out. I've said everything I have to say. So I just shuffle awkwardly and detonate the charges. The ground rumbles and shakes. A huge cloud of dust billows out of the entrance to the base, swallowing our little army whole.

For a moment, we are lost. Ghosts floating in a spectral world.

Then cannon fire rains down upon us.

32

———————

I dive for cover, rolling against a boulder. The cannon fire comes from nowhere and everywhere, streaking the dust cloud with green and blue light. They must have been watching us, waiting for the perfect time to strike.

"Shadow, have you got a fix on them?"

"Negative. The snipers are up above the cloud somewhere. We've got to get out of this dust."

"Everyone scramble," I shout over the general com. "This place is a deathtrap."

I dash toward where I think the Beast is, but get turned around in the dust and don't find it when I get there.

"Jmini, have you got a fix on the Beast?"

"Aye, Capitan. It's two hundred meters south." A map pops up on my retina display, a digital rendering of the canyon overlaying the swirling dust.

My stomach falls. I ran the wrong way. I'll never make it back to the Beast now.

I cast about for an alternative and see a dark vehicle looming up to my right. I run toward it, then skid to a halt. The vehicle is coming in my direction. Which means it's not leaving the dust, it's coming into it. Which means…

Cannon fire punches me off my feet, sending me sprawling in the dust. A familiar voice calls out.

"There he is. The man of the hour." Rory hops down from the transport and moves cautiously toward me, his silver armor caked with dust. He stops ten meters away, keeping his cannon trained on me. He knows I can beat him in a warpknife duel, and he's not taking any chances.

"Rory, did you do this? Did you slaughter all those people?"

His gun wavers. He glances away, his mouth twisting.

"Yeah, well … things got out of hand."

"They deserved to die." Ghengis steps around the vehicle, his armor a looming silhouette. His voice is thick with scorn. "If you live like a dog, you will die like a dog."

"Ghengis. I should have known it was you. Cruelty always was your style."

The giant moves toward me, his massive warpknife blazing red in his hand. "Your little girlfriend wants you captured alive, but accidents happen. Maybe I'll tell her you resisted arrest."

I scramble to my feet, drawing my own warpknife while my mind reels. Are Ghengis and Rory working for Kass? Did Kass order an entire Outsider base massacred? I can't believe she would do such a thing, but she is a Guardian. Like Shadow said, the Guardians follow orders. It could have been any of us in there.

Ghengis takes a vicious swing with his warpknife, trying to take my head off. I stumble back, caught off guard by the sudden attack. I've got to get out of my head, daydreaming will get me killed out here.

He presses the attack and I defend awkwardly, my missing eye affecting my depth perception. I retreat, trying to keep away from those massive hands. If he gets a grip on me, I'm done.

Wait, what am I doing? All those sparring sessions with Rust, and I forget everything the first time I'm in a real fight?

I open my sight.

Ghengis glows before me, a network of power running through his body. His right arm flares and I move a split second before he does, avoiding the blow. He lunges forward and I spin away.

The world slows around me, everything coming into sharp focus. This is just like practice. Like I'm sparring with Rust. I have to stay focused, understand what my opponent is going to do before he does.

I dance around Ghengis, flowing past his attacks. His power flares as his frustration mounts. I notice this in a detached, almost clinical way. As if I'm watching the fight from outside myself, seeing several moves ahead.

I parry an attack and move into the opening behind it, plunging the point of my warpknife into his shoulder. Ghengis bellows with rage and tries to cut me in half with a furious slice.

But I'm already gone, moving away before the attack even starts.

Warmth flows through me, and a fierce grin pushes my lips back. Ghengis can't touch me. I'm going to win this fight.

Then Rory shoots me in the face.

My visor stops the blast, but the force of it knocks me clean off my feet. I lie on my back in the dust, ears ringing, trying to stop the world from spinning.

"Not so fast now, are you?" Ghengis looms over me.

Kass's voice comes out of the dust. "Ghengis! Stand down!"

The scowling giant turns to face her. "He stabbed me."

"I'll stab you too if you don't back off." Kass glares at him, her eyes hard.

I notice she's pointing her cannon at him. That's interesting. Subordination in the ranks?

Ghengis stares at her for a long moment, then he turns and spits on the ground.

"Fine. You can keep your boyfriend."

He stalks away, joining Rory over by the vehicle, leaving Kass and me alone in the swirling dust.

I look up at her warily. "It looks like you've got me where you want me."

"Looks like it," Kass agrees. I notice her cannon is pointed at the ground, not at me.

"Did you do this?" I gesture toward the collapsed Outsider base. "Did you order this?"

Her face is stricken. "No! How could you even think that?"

"It's not exactly a big leap, based on the company you're keeping."

Her eyes dart to Ghengis and Rory.

"Yeah, well, you have to work with what you're given. The way my reputation suffered after you left, it's a miracle they put me in charge of anyone at all."

"So if you didn't do this, who did? The people who lived here were slaughtered. I saw grandparents with their intestines ripped out. Children with their skulls crushed. What kind of animals do something like that?"

Kass's lips press in a tight line. "They were Outsiders. They knew the risks."

"They were people, Kass! Families who only wanted to live their lives in peace!"

She glances at Ghengis and Rory again, then squats beside me. Her eyes are haunted. She keeps her voice low.

"They'd gone ahead to scout. They said they were ambushed, the Outsiders fired first. I didn't hear about it until it was all over. It's..." She takes a ragged breath. "It's unacceptable. Contemptible."

I lower my voice as well.

"This is why I'm helping the Outsiders, Kass. The Guardians are corrupt. They're not the good guys, they're the IEC's attack dogs. You have to see that."

She laughs bitterly.

"It doesn't make any difference what I think."

"But it could." I lean forward, practically whispering now. "We're going to bring down the IEC. You could help us. Do the right thing."

Kass arches an eyebrow at me.

"Oh, really? You're going to bring down the IEC? In case you haven't noticed, you're sitting on your butt in the dust with a bunch of Guardians pointing cannons at you. I don't think you're bringing anything down right now."

I hold her gaze.

"Think about it, Kass. You don't have to be like those murderers.

You and I both know there are good people in the Guardians too. They'd listen to you. You could make a difference. You can save lives."

The corner of Kass's mouth curls up as she shakes her head.

"You're dust-crazy, you know that? You've got a certifiable case of terminal optimism. I've got you captured and you're trying to talk me into defecting. Unbelievable."

"It's working isn't it? You're thinking about it. I can tell."

Kass glares at me. She's trying to look serious, but the corner of her mouth keeps quirking.

"I still owe you for dropping that scraphead on me."

"Me?" I'm all wide-eyed innocence. "I have no idea what you're talking about."

"Uh-huh."

"All right, maybe I did. But my intentions were good. If I hadn't buried you, that Forsaken would have torn you apart. I saved your life."

Kass purses her lips.

"Maybe. I'm willing to consider..."

Then there's a blur, and a crunch, and Kass is gone. In her place sits a black vehicle.

33

———

The door to the black vehicle pops open. Ianna leans out.

"Come on, Twist. Get in."

I whip my head around to where Kass lies sprawled in the dust. She groans, rolling onto her side. Even in her armor, that impact had to hurt. I hesitate, wanting to go help her up.

Rory and Ghengis make my decision for me, opening fire from the far side of the Forsaken vehicle. Cannon blasts splash around me like rain. I dive through the open door and the black vehicle lurches into motion.

The interior is unlike anything I've ever seen. There are no seats, just places where a passenger can squeeze in among the blocky machinery. The driver, Spanner, doesn't have a steering wheel. He's wired directly into the vehicle, a big cluster of cables runs through his headrest, plugging directly into the back of his skull. The instrument panel flares electric blue, mirroring the light in his eyes. He doesn't acknowledge my presence. I don't even know if he's aware of it.

I perch awkwardly on a flat piece of machinery. It hums under my legs. Ianna grins at me.

"Isn't this the sharpest thing ever?"

I manage a careful nod, my head still ringing from Rory's cannon blast.

"It's something else, all right." Under my breath, I say, "Jmini, does any of this make sense to you?"

"Certainly, Capitan. I recognize a number of things in this vehicle."

"A number? What number would that be?"

"I can confidently identify eleven point five percent of the mechanisms in my current field of perception."

My mouth opens, but no sound comes out. Eleven point five percent?

"So, you have no idea what almost eighty-nine percent of the machines in here do?"

"Eighty-eight point five percent."

"But you're an AI," I splutter. "Knowing things is your job!"

"There are more things in heaven and earth, Horatio,

Than are dreamt of in your philosophy."

"But..."

"Many more things."

I throw up my hands. "Fine. I get it. You're completely useless."

"Well, there's no need to be rude."

Jmini rattles on indignantly, but I've stopped listening. I gaze in wonder at the interior of the Forsaken vehicle. The carbon and steel housings. The electric blue instruments humming away with mysterious purposes, inscrutable as a boku hive.

I turn to Ianna.

"What are you doing in here?"

"It was the closest vehicle when the shooting started." She looks unconcerned.

"Spanner just let you in?"

She glances at me out of the corner of her eye.

"Yes. Why wouldn't he?"

"Because of all of this." I waggle my fingers around at the interior.

"What about it?"

"I mean, it's so alien."

Ianna raises an eyebrow at me.

Then I notice she's got some kind of Forsaken memory card sticking out of the hair behind her left ear.

"What are you doing, Ianna? Do you want to become one of them?"

She meets my gaze squarely.

"How is it any different than your Guardian implants, Twist? You've got an AI in your head. I've got a memory card. Which one of us is less human?"

"But my implants were put in by other humans!"

"Humans we're fighting against now. I hardly think that's an argument in their favor."

"I know but … you're my little sister," I finish lamely. I can't just drop it, even though I know I'm in the wrong.

Ianna reaches out and takes my hand, her fingers warm against mine. It's the first time she's voluntarily touched me since we extracted her from the Carlyle estate.

"And you'll always be my big brother. But you're not my dad. I'm old enough to make my own decisions."

"Are you?" I squint at her dubiously.

She rolls her eyes and lets my hand drop.

"Stop worrying. This feels right. Trust me, ok?"

I take a deep breath and let it hiss away between my teeth. I examine her face, so much older than the Ianna I remember, yet still so young. Is she really old enough to make such a big decision?

It's her eyes that finally convince me. The anger that's been covering their surface isn't gone, but it has receded. Like silt settling to the bottom of a pool after a flood has passed. For the first time since I've gotten her back, Ianna looks happy and inquisitive again. Excited to be alive.

I think about the way she used to remember everything when we were kids. How she could put the pieces of a game back exactly where they'd fallen, even days later. Is it so hard to believe a mind like that would recognize cyborgs as kindred spirits?

I swallow my fears and my pride.

"OK, Ianna. I trust you."

Her smiles lights up the interior of the vehicle. Despite the surroundings and the weird Forsaken tech in her skull, I almost feel like I have my sister back.

I peer out the small window. Other Forsaken vehicles are out there, racing with us. I'm surprised to discover we've already left the ambush and the dust cloud behind. This thing moves fast.

I crane my neck to look back. The dusty canyon is small in the distance. I think I see Guardians on the rim, but I can't be sure.

Kass was in command of that squad. Doesn't that mean she's responsible for what happened back there at the Outsider base? For all those deaths?

She said it happened before she got there. But aren't all commanders ultimately responsible for the actions of their troops?

I remember the shame on Rory's face as he said, "Things got out of hand."

Shadow's words come right behind them. Guardians follow orders. It could have been any of us.

34

———————

"I don't know, Twist. I think we've got to come up with a better plan. Something smells off to me." Shadow paces around the map, frowning.

We're gathered in a cave less than two kilometers outside the perimeter. Distance is subjective when you're dealing with the scablands, though. In a flier, we're less than two kilometers. On the ground, we're three canyons and several thousand vertical meters away from the fence line. The odds of a Guardian patrol stumbling upon us are low.

That doesn't make me any less nervous. We're planning the largest assault Canyon City's ever seen. Thousands of people are counting on me. Thousands could die if I get it wrong.

"I think that smell is Knott's feet." My joke falls flat, and I duck my head. "Sorry."

"We'd better figure out what's not working." Tempest's projection flickers atop a tripod. "We only get one shot at this."

I nod miserably.

Shadow was finally able to get in touch with Tempest. The Forsaken boosted the signal on her com gear to reach the deep base the remaining Outsiders are hiding in.

"So what's off?" I look at Shadow expectantly.

"I don't know. That's the problem."

I throw up my hands. "Well until you figure it out, we'll have to proceed as planned."

"Yeah." She sighs and rubs her temples. "I think I've been staring at this map too long."

"You and me both."

We've been hunched over the map for hours, planning, arguing, scrapping plans, and making new plans. In addition to me, Shadow, and Tempest, our war council includes Ianna, Rust, Spanner, and Knott.

Ianna catches my eye across the cavern and smiles. Aside from Spanner, she's the calmest person here. She stays close to the Forsaken leader, like she's drawing on his aura or something.

My lips press into a thin line as my eye shifts to the black carbon figure beside her. I can't shake the feeling that he's got ulterior motives. Spanner argued in favor of helping us in the Forsaken council chamber even before Ianna beat him at the pyramid game. He wanted to be here, and Ianna beating him just gave him the excuse he needed to defy the council. But why? What does he really gain by helping us?

On the other hand, if my sister has shown me anything, it's that I don't understand the Forsaken at all. Maybe the pyramid game really is that important to them. Maybe they just have a machinelike obsession with truth.

I rub my eyes and force myself to turn back to the map. I'm dust-gathering. Avoiding the main topic.

"Shadow, did you get the footage of the massacre to Grab?"

"Yes, it's been transmitting all over Canyon City. People are angry. Everyone in Canyon City has some connection to the Outsiders. Friends or family who have run away. They don't like seeing them slaughtered. There have already been confrontations in the street; crowds yelling at Guardians on patrol."

"Good. Tell Grab to keep transmitting. We need to stoke that fire. Keep the Guardians distracted while we sneak in and do some damage."

"Maybe we're not thinking big enough," Tempest says suddenly. "What if we hit the city at the same time as you?"

I gape at her. "You've been getting pounded for weeks and you want to fight back now?"

"We've been itching to hit the Guardians for years. This could be the chance we've been waiting for. Once you start blowing things up in the transport yard, the wall will be left with a skeleton crew of defenders. If you can get the gate open, we can catch them by surprise. We might even be able to take control of the city."

"You think we can take the whole city?" I rock back on my heels. "This is based on your extensive success fighting the Guardians the last few weeks?"

"No need to get snarky, Twist," Shadow jumps in. "It's a crazy idea, but she's not wrong. Your message has got people angry; public opinion is with us. You've inspired them so much they've even given you a nickname. I hear they're calling you the Cyclops."

"Cyclops? Seriously?" I wince and rub the skin beside my eyepatch self-consciously.

"Canyon City is lightly defended right now," Tempest says. "Most of the Guardians are outside the wall, trying to dig us out of our bunkers. If we can get behind them and get a force inside the city, we might have a chance. There's never been a better time for a revolution."

Rust clears his throat.

"It's an intriguing idea. If we can eliminate their numbers advantage and take them by surprise, we've got a chance. We could cut off the head of the snake in one clean motion. Momentum is a powerful thing in a battle. Timing is crucial. It sounds like you've already captured the public imagination, Cyclops. Maybe we should ride that wave and see how far it takes us."

I stare at them, my mind whirling. Suddenly we're not content with making the Guardians pull back inside the wall. Now we want to bring down the entire governing council of Canyon City.

All of this with a handful of Guardian deserters, a hundred Forsaken, a few Hubzoh, and the sad remnants of the Outsiders. Jelly easy, right?

Well, isn't that what I told the people in the vid? That we were going to bring down the IEC and free everyone? I didn't think it was going to happen so soon, but…

I take a deep breath and square my shoulders.

"All right, why not? There's no time like the present. Carpe diem and all that. Let's get to work. We've got a revolution to plan."

35

———

The cavern is smaller than I remember it being. Or maybe that's just because there are more people in it now: Our raiding party stretches into the darkness behind me. But the greicagins embedded in the walls still sparkle, making my skin tingle.

"This is where we first met Akona," I subvocalize.

"You mean the place where you thought it would be a good idea to try and pet a Rock Horror," Jmini says. "I should have known right then you were completely round-the-bend, Cyclops."

"Don't you start with the Cyclops stuff too. And I was not completely round-the-bend. I turned out to be right about the Hubzoh, didn't I?"

"Speaking of which, where is that creature anyway? We haven't seen her in days."

"That's a good question. Hey Rust, where's your pet monster?"

The old Guardian gives me a sidelong look.

"Pet monster?"

"Don't be difficult. You know who I mean. Where are Akona and her friends?"

"Did passing through this cavern again remind you of her existence?"

"Yes. Now stop trying to change the subject."

The corner of his mouth quirks up.

"Me? Change the subject?"

"And there you go again."

Rust laughs, and I tense at the sound. His merriment seems out of place underground. When I was a deep diver in Papa Grady's camp, they taught us to never make loud noises underground, for fear of attracting Horrors. Some habits die hard.

The old warrior sidles up to me and lowers his voice. "She's nearby. I told her to stay out of sight. Our alliance with the Forsaken seems delicate enough without their dislike of the Hubzoh stirring them up."

"That makes sense. But she's nearby, if you need her? I have a feeling this fight is going to need all hands on deck."

Rust's expression sobers. "Yes, she is. And she has friends with her. But we should only use the Hubzoh as a last resort."

"Why?"

"Think about it. How will the average person in Canyon City react if the Hubzoh start attacking Guardians in the street? Do you think they'll want the Hubzoh to win?"

"Good point. That could turn public opinion against us in a hurry."

"Exactly, and we need the public with us to have any hope of success. The Hubzoh will support us if we really need them, but it will be best if we don't need them."

"Right. I'll keep that in mind."

I chew my lip as we wind our way through the cavern. Shadow, Rust, Tempest, and Spanner are all brilliant tacticians and fighters, and they've all helped to make a solid battle plan. But no plan ever goes off exactly the way you expect, and once things launch they're counting on me to coordinate everything in real time. To improvise and keep all the separate pieces of the assault working together in a coherent strategy.

It's a lot of pressure, and a lot of lives are riding on my decisions. Maybe every life in Canyon City.

My heart constricts in my chest. I can't breathe.

It's too much. I can't do this. I can't be in charge of the fate of thousands of people.

"Breathe, Twist," Jmini says in my ear.

"It's too big," I gasp.

"Don't think about the big picture. Keep it small. Focus on your breath. In and out. Let the air flow down your throat. Fill your lungs. Nice and easy. In and out."

I do my best to follow his instructions. To stop thinking and focus on the simple physical mechanism of breathing. My body is an automated machine. It will do what it needs to if I can get my mind out of the way. Stop thinking and just breathe. Let my body do the work.

Slowly, the tightness in my chest loosens. My throat opens.

I find Shadow watching me.

"Are you all right?"

"Yeah. Fine."

I start to walk away, but she stops me, forcing me to meet her eyes.

"You've got this. This isn't any harder than our final exam at Merrimac. And we survived that just fine."

I laugh. "Right. Ask Grab how he feels about your definition of 'fine'."

"Are the Outsiders fine right now? Are the people of Canyon City fine?"

"No, but…"

"We're their only hope, Twist. If we don't win this fight, it'll be a hundred years before anyone dares to resist the IEC again. More generations living and dying to fill some corporate balance sheet."

"I know. Why do you think I'm so worried? This isn't like school. I only had five people counting on me then. Now it's thousands. That's a lot of pressure."

"One step at a time, Twist. Nobody can run a thousand kilometers, but anyone can take one step. One foot in front of the other."

"One foot in front of the other," I repeat.

"Don't worry. We've got your back." Shadow smiles and Knott puts her hand on my shoulder.

I get a lump in my throat as I do my best to smile back. Shadow and Knott are my crew. My best friends. I think about all the things we've been through together since our first day in Merrimac, all the obstacles we've overcome. We were never supposed to get this far.

They never wanted us to graduate Merrimac, never expected us to become Guardians at all.

The stakes are higher now: higher than I ever imagined they could get. But we overcame everything they threw at us, and here we are, still standing. Still fighting. If I'm going to do impossible things today, there's nobody I'd rather have with me.

As we start moving again, I think about how weird it is, leading a small army through these caverns. The last time I was down here it was just Jmini and me chasing Jepet, following a blue dot on my retina map through dark, empty tunnels.

Now the walls echo with the clank of shifting armor and weapons, the tromping of hundreds of feet. Every reverberation magnifies the sound, turning each of us into dozens, making our little force roar like an avalanche.

If only it were that easy.

We halt in the small cavern outside Jepet's cellar, the stalactites glowing in my nightvision. The door looks unchanged from this side.

I lean in close to Shadow.

"Do you think he's still in there?"

She shrugs. "He's a fool if he is. But it wouldn't surprise me. It could be some kind of macho thing to prove he's not afraid of us."

I motion Knott over. She's got four Forsaken warriors with her, their blocky augments sparking in the dark. I wish I could give her a better-trained force, but you work with the soldiers you have, not the ones you wish you had. As long as the Forsaken's interests stay aligned with ours, they should be reliable. They're certainly fierce enough fighters.

"Are you ready to kick in the door?"

The big girl gives me a grin. "I am ready."

I clap her on the shoulder as I turn to face the others, trying to project a confidence I don't feel. I catch their eyes one by one: Ianna, Shadow, Rust, and Spanner.

"All right, everyone, it's time to do this. May the sun be at your back."

The time for talk is over.

36

The door explodes inward, the blast deafening in the small cavern. The streaked afterimage of Knott's cannon lingers across my retina.

Knott and her crew are moving before the echoes fade, storming through the doorway. Indignant shouts greet them, followed by more cannon fire. I squeeze the handle of my warpknife, fighting the urge to charge in after them. I can't do everything myself. Part of being a leader is letting other people do their jobs.

Knott proves my faith in her is sound, stomping out all resistance in two minutes flat. The shouts and cannon fire go silent, and her voice crackles in my earcone.

"All clear."

I step through the doorway and find the large bedchamber I remember. Only this time it's not Jepet standing against the wall with his hands raised. It's a woman, tall and thin, all wiry muscles and scars beneath her black bra and underwear.

I stare at the woman for a moment, recognition tickling the back of my mind. Then a chill grips my spine.

"Zetta?"

It's been years since the last time I saw her, but the Crystal Clan's hunter hasn't changed at all. She's still whip-thin, her hair shaved up to a point on top of her head.

The Crystal Clan controlled the scrapyards in my section of Canyon City when I was younger. In fact, I scavenged Jmini from one of their yards. Zetta was their most feared enforcer. We only spoke her name in whispers.

Her eyes are cold and deadly as they latch onto me.

"Whoever you are, you're dead," she promises, her voice flat.

"Where's Jepet?" I ignore her threat.

She looks puzzled. "Jepet? How should I know?"

Now it's my turn to be confused.

"Isn't this his complex?"

"No. This place belongs to the Crystal Clan. To me. And you're trespassing."

"What happened to Jepet?"

"He abandoned this place. I took it over."

"Well in that case, I apologize for the inconvenience. We need to move a large force through your bedroom. Sit tight and we'll be out of your hair shortly."

I give the signal and the Forsaken start filing through the room behind me.

Zetta's eyes go wide at the parade of cyborgs. "What the dust?"

"Relax, we're not your enemies. In fact," I look at her speculatively, "we could be friends."

"I'm not friends with Guardians."

"I'm not a Guardian."

Zetta cocks an eyebrow. "Oh, really? That looks like Guardian armor you're wearing to me."

I look down at myself and smile sheepishly.

"Yeah, it does, doesn't it? It's true, I was a Guardian, however briefly. But I started out as a rockhead, just like you. Becoming a Guardian was only a means to an end."

"And what end was that?"

"To find my sister, and make her safe. The first part wasn't so hard. The second part … well, that's gotten complicated."

Zetta just looks at me, arms crossed over her bare stomach. She's starting to shiver, so I toss her one of the blankets from her bed.

"Thank you." She wraps the blanket around her shoulders. "You were saying?"

"The short answer is that I've discovered there's nowhere safe for a rockhead on this planet, not really. Not as long as the IEC is in charge."

Zetta eyes me skeptically. "You're that Cyclops everyone's yelling about. You think you're going to change that?"

"I am. The IEC has profited from our blood and sweat long enough. We're taking back Canyon City. Now is your chance to be part of the new order. The Crystal Clan can get in on the ground floor."

"What are you doing, Twist?" Jmini whispers in my ear. "The Crystal Clan is dangerous. I would know; I used to work for them before you found me."

"What's that old saying?" I subvocalize. "Better the devil you know? Besides, the Clan have strong fighters. We can use every soldier we can get right now."

"You can't trust them. They're only out for themselves."

"That's true. But that also makes them predictable. As long as it's in their best interest to help us, they will."

Zetta taps her finger against her forearm, her eyes narrow with thought.

"Circulating that vid of the Outsider massacre was a clever move. You've got the whole city riled up. Public opinion has always been mixed when it comes to the Outsiders, but thanks to your footage, Canyon City feels like a kettle about to boil."

She watches the stream of Forsaken passing behind me, her eyes calculating.

"Strange allies you've got."

"The revolution takes all kinds."

She grins, a thin, knife-edge slit that exposes no teeth.

"So I've noticed." Her eyes flick from me to the Forsaken and back again. Finally, she nods. "OK. We're not going to take orders from you, but any place we can take down Guardians, we will."

Zetta extends her hand. I step forward and clasp it. Her skin is cold and dry, like polished stone.

"How will we know when it's time to move?" she asks.

Now it's my turn to grin.

"Keep your ears open, you'll know. The whole city will know."

37

——————

Once we hit the streets, we have to move fast. We've planned our attack for the middle of the night, but still, the second someone sees a column of Forsaken running down the street, there's going to be screaming.

The attack has three parts. First, we're going to blow up the transportation yard. Originally, we were going to do this so the Guardians would pull their soldiers back inside the wall, out of the scablands. Now we don't care about that. In fact, we want most of the Guardians to stay outside the wall. If we can get our troops inside Canyon City while keeping theirs out, that's half the battle right there.

So what's the point of blowing up the transportation yard then?

Simple.

The yard is on the far side of the city, away from the main gate. The Guardians will go running for the yard when they hear the explosion. That will leave a skeleton crew at the gate.

And that's when we launch the second prong of our attack.

While the transportation yard bombing crew keeps the Guardians busy, our second force will hit the main gate. The gate is designed to keep people outside of the wall, not in, so we'll be hitting it from the side that's hard to defend. If everything goes according to plan, we'll overwhelm the skeleton crew and throw the gates open, allowing the Outsiders' army to pour into Canyon City.

Then it's time for step three. My step.

While the Guardians are busy defending the city on two fronts, my crew and I are going after Julius.

Yes, I know it didn't work out the last time we tried to kill Julius. But this time there will be serious distractions. With all the fighting in the streets, nobody's going to be looking in our direction. We'll slip in and cut the head off the snake in one smooth stroke. Jelly easy. What could possibly go wrong?

"I'm going to assume that's a rhetorical question," Jmini says. "Otherwise we'll be here all night while I count the ways."

"I'm trying to keep a positive outlook, Jmini. You're not helping."

"My apologies. I didn't realize that lying to yourself was an essential element of your plan."

"Well, it is. Remember that whole thousand-kilometer journey, one-step-at-a-time thing? If I don't lie to myself, I'll never even get to step one."

"And after all, what is a lie? 'Tis but the truth in masquerade."

"Exactly. I'm having a fancy truth dress-up party."

"I always knew you secretly yearned for fancy dress. Perhaps we can get a tuxedo and tails. Or a doublet and hose. Or even a toga!"

I sigh and run my hands over my face. Sometimes talking to Jmini is like falling face-first down a crevasse.

I turn to the rest of the team.

"Anyone have any final questions?"

"When the revolution is over, can I be in charge of rebuilding the communications network?" Grab's voice comes from everywhere and nowhere. "I had no idea how antiquated it was until I had to hack it to spread that massacre video. Some of those terminals are nearly a hundred years old! There's more dust in the junction boxes than there are gladiators in the old quarry."

I smile. It's good to have our eye-in-the-sky back on the job.

"Grab, if you get us through this night in one piece, you can have any job you want."

"Oh, in that case maybe I should set my sights higher."

"Don't push your luck. Anyone else?"

I look at my lieutenants gathered around me. Shadow, Knott, Rust, and Ianna. The people I trust more than anyone in the world.

As my eyes settle on my sister, my mouth turns down. She looks ridiculous in her mismatched gear: part salvaged Outsider armor and part custom-fabricated carbon plates Spanner made for her. Her too-big helmet keeps falling over her eyes.

I tried to get her to stay behind, but she wouldn't listen. She said we all had to fight to make a new future, every single one of us. If the future of Canyon City is going to be decided today, she wants to be in the thick of it.

And I guess that's part of growing up, right? Making your own decisions and living with the consequences. As Dad would have said, you have to do the right thing, no matter the cost.

Ianna smiles sadly at me, as if she's reading my thoughts.

"I miss him too. This is for Dad."

I force the corners of my mouth up and give her a little nod.

"Yeah. For Dad."

I check in with the others, one by one.

Knott lifts me in a bear hug, squeezing me with the arms of her massive power armor. "Be safe out there, Twist."

"You too, Knott," I gasp. I wince as she puts me down. I think she might have cracked a rib.

Rust gives me a salute.

"You're ready for this, General. Lead us to victory."

I return the salute solemnly. "Yessir, Captain Steel."

Rust's eyes widen at my use of his former name. He coughs and looks down, studying his toes.

I face Shadow last. The bravest person I know. My best friend. The one who has stood beside me from the very beginning.

I want to tell her all of these things, and more.

"Shadow, I..."

She places a finger over my lips.

"I know," she says simply. "Save it for after the battle. Right now we've got a revolution to win."

38

———————

The transportation yard is the biggest open space in Canyon City, stretching silent and dark beneath a thousand sparkling stars. The edge of the horizon is just starting to lighten with the coming dawn. My breath steams in the crisp air, my face feeling brittle in the cold.

"I count two guards," Shadow whispers over the com.

"There's two more on the far side of the yard," Grab corrects, using his drones' eye-in-the-sky perspective.

"The far side of the yard is five hundred meters away, so I doubt they'll be a factor," I say. "It's the ones on this side we need to worry about. Can we take them out without killing them? I'd rather not have civilian casualties if we can avoid it."

Shadow cocks her head.

"Probably, but we'll have to get closer than if we were just going to shoot them. Might give them time to sound the alarm."

"Would that be a bad thing?" I ask. "The whole point of this is to create a distraction that will bring the Guardians running. Wouldn't an alarm help us?"

"Not if it goes off before we plant the charges." I can almost hear Shadow rolling her eyes.

"Right. OK, you plant the charges on this end. I'll take care of the guards and do the east side."

"Whatever you say, Cyclops."

I grimace at my new name and keep my head down as I creep around the perimeter of the fence. I could have probably strolled up whistling; the guards are huddled inside their little heated post, door shut tight against the cold. One of them watches a vid. The other is slumped in his chair, trailing a string of drool from his bottom lip, asleep. They're not wearing armor, and their cannons are hanging on straps beside the door. The tiny hut would make pointing my cannon at them awkward.

So I draw my warpknife instead.

"Hands where I can see them." I step through the door and level the tip of my blade at the one watching the vid.

He turns with a surly look on his face, but his eyes get big when he sees the warpknife. He raises his hands.

"Secure Sleeping Beauty here to his chair," I say.

The guard grabs a roll of sealant and starts to wrap it around his partner. As he squats to do the man's ankles, an explosion shatters the quiet.

"Shadow? What was that?" I peer out into the night.

The guard takes the opportunity to drive his shoulder into my stomach.

I grunt as my back slams against the side of the hut. The guard is heavier than I am, and he's got his legs braced. I awkwardly try to wrestle him around the shoulders, but I'm trying not to hurt the guy, so I'm only using the arm that's not holding my warpknife. It's not going well. He's got all the leverage, and there's no room to maneuver in the tiny hut.

His partner starts awake. He tries to stand, but his half-tied legs trip him up and he falls toward the cannons. He still manages to yank one off its hook on the way down.

Spines. This is getting out of hand.

I slam the hilt of my warpknife into the skull of the guard pinning me to the wall. It loosens his grip, so I do it a couple more times. He falls to the floor, groaning.

His partner shoots me with his cannon.

The close-range blast kicks my chest plate hard, knocking the wind out of me.

I curse and lash out with my warpknife, shearing the barrel off the cannon. The guard drops it like a hot rock, raising his hands.

"Don't hurt me. I've got a family."

"That's what I was trying not to do in the first place," I snap. "Before your friend here decided to be a hero. Sit down and put your hands behind you."

I finish wrapping him with sealant tape, then do the same to the guard on the floor.

The guard in the chair creases his brow at me. "Who are you? You're not a Guardian."

"No, I'm one of the good guys. We've been slaves to the IEC long enough. That ends today."

His eyes get wide. "You're that Cyclops guy from the vid."

I nod. "Yeah, I guess I am."

"I saw that footage of the massacre. That was an ugly business. For what it's worth, I hope you win. Those bastards have been profiting off our blood long enough."

"Thanks. If it comes down to fighting in the streets, I hope you remember who the good guys are."

I leave the guards bound and step back out into the night.

"Shadow? Is everything all right?"

"Under control," she grunts.

"What was that explosion?"

"One of the timers malfunctioned. Dust-sucking bomb almost went off in my hand."

"Are you OK?"

"Fine. I'm almost finished rigging up the rest of the charges. Take care of your end and we'll see some real fireworks."

"It's not going to be that easy," Grab interrupts. "That explosion woke up the other guards."

I turn and see two beams of light making their way across the yard. Spines.

"I'm on it," I say. "Shadow, you take care of the charges."

"Roger that."

With this set of guards already awake, there's no point in being stealthy. I charge in hard and fast, sprinting across the rail lines. The guards hit me with their cannons a couple of times before I get to them, but my black armor shrugs it off. My warpknife makes short work of their cannons.

"Put your hands in the air and nobody gets hurt."

The guards do as I say. They're just rockhead security guards. Handling me is above their pay grade.

By the time I get the guards secured and get back to Shadow, she's finished placing the charges. Above us, dawn streaks the sky with orange fingers.

Shadow grins at me. "Do you want to do the honors?"

"No, you placed the charges. You should do it."

She pauses, her finger poised, breath steaming in the rising light.

"I feel like I should say something."

"One small step for man?" I suggest.

She rolls her eyes.

"How about, *Viva la revolución*?"

I grin.

"Viva la revolución."

Her finger comes down. The dawn explodes.

39

The explosion is impressive, shooting a fireball so high I swear it touches the orange clouds. The blast echoes off the canyon walls for long seconds.

"Well," I say as we listen to the rumble fade, "that'll wake everyone up."

On cue, lights flicker on in the spires all around us. Silhouettes of sleepy people poke their heads out of windows.

"That's stirred the pot," Grab confirms. "I detect alarms in all of the Guardians' posts."

"Time to move," I say. "We don't want to be here when the Guardians arrive."

Shadow and I pound down the dusty streets. We take the back alleys, winding between the hollowed-out spires. The Guardians will be rushing toward the transportation yard, and we're better off not running into them on the way.

It takes almost ten minutes for us to cross the city. Plenty of time for the Guardians to scramble out to the transportation yard. We left a handful of the Forsaken there to keep the Guardians distracted while we go after our real objective.

My pulse pounds as I run, my heart singing with terror and wild joy. This is it; we're finally taking the fight to the IEC. This is the day I finish what my dad started.

Of course, it's not going to be easy. This becomes abundantly clear as we round the final corner and come upon the battle for the wall already in full swing.

The Forsaken batter the doors to the interior of the wall, trying to get inside, where they can use their strength and speed. These interior doors should be easier to break through than the big, fortified gate on the outside of the wall, but still, the Guardians aren't making things easy for us. The defenders lean out over the edge, dropping a steady rain of cannon fire from the top of the wall. But I can tell the Guardians are undermanned. There should be four times as many cannons firing up there. It looks like our distraction worked to perfection.

The Forsaken wheel a huge cutting machine up to one of the doors. It takes four of them to maneuver it into place. The cannon fire raining down upon them makes me think of battering rams and medieval siege engines. Invaders at the gate.

The blade of the machine flares blue, so bright I have to shield my eyes. The tip pierces the reinforced door and starts slicing downward —no mean feat. I've been inside that door, and it's nearly a meter thick.

The Guardians redouble their efforts, pouring everything they've got into stopping the huge blade. Two of the Forsaken holding the machine fall away, their bodies sparking in the half-light. But two more step in to take their place, and the machine does not slow.

With a crash, the enormous door falls in, hitting the ground with a thump so deep I feel it in my feet. A clump of Guardians stand exposed within, spotless and shining in their silver armor, warpknives blazing. The Forsaken rush them, pushing them back inside, and the battle for the wall is joined in earnest.

Shadow and I charge for the opening and pass into the wall half a step behind Knott. The big tank is in her element, pushing aside Guardians like lanbrush. She tries the elevator, but the defenders have disabled it. We're going to have to take the stairs.

Stairs are some of the least favorable terrain for an attack. The defenders have the high ground, and can fire and drop things down on you at will. Every landing is a built-in defensive platform, and the attackers have to take these fortified positions over and over. Climbing two floors against determined defenders can be suicide. We have to climb eight.

Luckily, every Forsaken is pretty much a tank. I'm astounded at the damage they absorb as we ascend, and they seem to have no fear or sense of self-preservation. Every time one of them falls, two more step forward to take their place. The Guardians pour down fire, but the Forsaken still climb, step by inexorable step.

My breath catches as I see Ianna in their midst, with Spanner beside her. With her carbon armor, she looks just like one of the cyborgs. But she's not, she's my little sister. She doesn't belong here. She should be somewhere safe.

I push through the crowd until I reach her side.

"Ianna, you shouldn't be in the middle of this." I have to yell to be heard over the clamor of battle.

"This is my fight too, Twist. This fight belongs to every person in Canyon City. I'm not going to sit on the sideline just because my big brother is worried about me."

"But..."

Spanner puts a heavy black hand on my shoulder.

"I will keep her safe. You have my word." His blue eyes burn, the heat sinks on his head flexing and straightening.

I'm not sure if his pronouncement makes me feel better or not. I look from his electric eyes to my sister's determined ones. Their shape reminds me of our dad's.

This was Dad's fight. And Ianna is right: This is everyone's fight, really. She has as many reasons to be here as anyone else does. More, really, considering what Julius did to her. And to Dad.

I take a deep breath. I have to let Ianna go again. I thought I already made peace with her making her own decisions, but here I am, working to accept it one more time.

Maybe that's just life. Maybe you never stop wanting to protect the people you love. Maybe you have to force yourself to step away every time. Allow them to make their own decisions, even if those decisions make you scared or uncomfortable.

I look into my sister's eyes and force a smile.

"Be careful. You're a pain in the spine, but you're the only sister I have."

She smirks.

"You too. May the sun be at your back, Twist."

Then we're climbing again, and the time for words has passed.

A pair of Forsaken collapse into smoking heaps on the fifth floor landing right in front of me. I start to get worried. The Forsaken are formidable, but they're a limited resource. We only had about a hundred total. We might be down to half, and we still haven't gotten the exterior gate open to let in the Outsiders.

I'm afraid our assault is taking too long. Have the Guardians that went running to the transportation yard figured out it was a diversion? How long until they come back and start cutting us up from the rear?

"Shadow, Knott, with me."

I duck out onto the fifth floor. Aside from a trio of fallen Guardians, the hallway is empty. I glance down at the lifeless faces and freeze. Staring up at me is Dez, one of the kids from our training class in Merrimac. I didn't know him well, but he seemed like one of the decent ones. Now he's dead.

I grind my teeth and clench my fists tight.

Shadow lays a hand on my shoulder.

"It's war, Twist. There's going to be casualties."

"I know." I wipe the back of my fist across my eyes. "That doesn't make it any easier."

"No," she agrees quietly. "It doesn't."

I tear myself away from the corpse and sprint down the hall. If we don't get the wall open, all these deaths will be for nothing.

I find the entrance to another stairwell and peer through the door onto a deserted landing. It's dark and quiet, just as I'd hoped. Everyone is in the other stairwell.

"Come on, quickly." I start to step out, but Knott pushes past me.

"I am Tank. I go first."

The corners of my mouth push up. "Absolutely. After you, m'lady."

Knott "hmphs" and steps onto the first stair.

We climb quickly and quietly, taking turns securing each landing, leapfrogging each other as we go. All we find is darkness.

At the eighth floor landing, we pause.

"OK," I whisper. "This is it. The control room is about a hundred meters down on the left. If our luck holds, everyone will be concentrating on the other stairwell and we can sneak up behind them."

I extend three fingers in the air.

Opening the door in three.

Two.

One.

40
____

We're half a dozen steps into the hallway when it all goes sideways. Cannon fire lights us up, filling the hall with sizzling bursts of energy. We duck and sprint for the nearest doorway.

Then more fire starts to hit us in the back.

"Crossfire!" I yell. "They're behind us too!"

Knott grunts.

Shadow curses. "I knew this was too easy."

We slide into an open doorway, getting out of the worst of the fire. Knott and I pop our cannons in and out, returning fire while Shadow fiddles with her instruments.

Her mouth turns down, and she growls in frustration.

"There are six behind us, and a dozen ahead in the control room. Now we know why it was so easy to get up that stairwell. They were waiting for us."

"How's our main force doing?" I ask.

"Not good. The Forsaken assault has stalled two floors down. It doesn't look like they're getting any higher. On top of that, Grab says our diversion at the transportation yard has run its course. The Guardians' main force is heading back this way."

I slam my fist down in frustration. "We've got to get the gate open.

The Outsiders will get destroyed if the Guardians are up here waiting for them. We've got to let them inside the city where they can fight street-to-street. How long until the Guardians' main force gets back here?"

Shadow consults her map. "Ten minutes, if we're lucky."

I chew my lip, thinking furiously.

"Ok, we've got to move. We don't have time to do this properly, so quick and dirty is our only option. Shadow, pull up your covert cloak. Here's what we're going to do."

Knott and I start by launching a flight of snapdragon missiles in both directions. Using the noise and smoke they create as a distraction, we slide a handful of disruption mines out after them.

Then we charge.

We ignore the team behind us and go directly for the control room. Hopefully the snapdragons and disruption mines buy us enough time that we don't get ground to gravel sprinting up the hall.

Knott leads, and I hunch down right behind her. Shadow pads softly in our wake, silent and invisible beneath her covert cloak.

Cannon fire splashes off Knott's heavy armor like dust in a storm, scorching black circles into the walls and ceiling. Moving in this way lets her armor shrug off most of the damage and also shields me from view, allowing me a moment of surprise when we enter the control room and I leap out with my warpknife blazing.

Cannons are no match for a warpknife in close quarters. I cut down two Guardians before they can react, and the third barely dodges my first strike. Then they get their own warpknives out, and things get dangerous in a hurry.

I shift my focus to my blind eye, and the world shimmers red, glowing with fields of greicagin energy.

Knott is a blazing bonfire beside me. Half a dozen Guardians scramble to form a ring around her. As I watch, one misjudges her massive reach and Knott's warpknife catches him across the chest. He won't make that mistake again.

Still, Knott has to fight defensively now. Her heavy armor may be impervious to cannon fire, but against warpknives she's as vulnerable as everyone else. She steps back, putting her back to the wall so they can't surround her.

I've got four Guardians facing me. Like Knott, I fall into a defensive crouch, watching the energy shift and flow in my attackers. To my right, a man's arm flares for a half-second before he strikes. I lunge left, and the tip of his warpknife passes centimeters from my ribs.

Unfortunately, this puts me within reach of the woman on my left. She stabs so quickly I barely have time to register the strike. I twist, parrying desperately, and deflect her knife just enough so that it scrapes a long gash across the plating over my belly button instead of dragging out my intestines. It's a close thing, though, and I scramble back out of range before any of the others can strike.

I've never tried to use my greicagin sight against multiple attackers before, and the strain of tracking the movements of four people at once is making me dizzy. I backpedal, waving my warpknife in front of me in a wild effort to keep my attackers out of range. Following Knott's example, I retreat until my heels strike the base of the wall.

Sensing weakness, the four Guardians spread out and close in.

Knott seems to be doing better than I am. Out of the corner of my eye, I see a short, powerfully built man get a little too close with one of his attacks. Knott latches onto his wrist and jerks him forward, slamming his faceplate into the wall. As the other Guardians step in to take advantage of her distraction, she hauls the unfortunate man off his feet and swings him like an armored club. His body whips before her in a flat arc, slamming into a pair of her attackers with bone-cracking force, sending all three tumbling to the floor.

Grinning, Knott waggles her warpknife toward her remaining attackers. They all take a step back.

Then my quartet is coming at me again, and I need all my focus to stay alive.

If I pause to think, I'll be dead—so I let all conscious thought go, becoming a creature of pure reaction. Reading the energy flares of my assailants, I move before my conscious mind even registers their attacks, parrying and dodging, staying millimeters ahead of death.

My heart beats as I suck in a breath. My balance shifts, knees bend, shoulder pivots.

I exhale. Sweat runs down my temple. My warpknife scrapes another, blade against blade, a finger's breadth from my throat. I spin away.

Time slows down, moving forward frame by frame. Click, pause, move. I inhabit each moment, understanding and reacting within the greicagin flow. Muscles contracting. Breath hissing between my teeth. The clashes and clangs of battle distant in my ears. Click, pause, move.

Then an alarm blares, and all of four of my opponents flare like cannon fire. They stutter, half turning, distracted by the noise.

I slip into the opening like a reaper spine on the wind. Thrust, slice, pivot. Two of them fall before the others even register my movement.

I lunge. The third folds over, the handle of my warpknife protruding from their chestplate.

The fourth keeps their head and leaps back, coolly defending.

But their advantage is gone. Now it's one against one.

I press in, still in the zone. Feint high, feint low, pivot.

A clean diagonal slice up across the ribs, and my last opponent falls.

I spin, searching for my next foe. All I find is Knott and a room full of fallen Guardians.

Shadow leans over the control panel, her covert cloak dropped. While we were keeping the guards busy, she's been working on the gate controls. A big red light flashes on the wall above her head. A recorded voice comes over the speaker.

"The gate is opening. All personnel stand clear. The gate is opening."

41

———

S hadow looks up and grins.

"Good distraction. You did more than just keep them all busy."

I look at the Guardians sprawled on the floor around us. My eyes grow wide—Knott and I just took out a dozen Guardians.

Behind Shadow, the display shows the massive gates swinging open. Pink and orange dawn streaks the sky overhead. The light hasn't reached the ground yet, and the scablands beyond the wall are a vast grey murk.

In that murk, something flashes. A glint of metal, answered by another glint twenty meters to the side. A hint of movement catches my eye, like ripples beneath a sheet. The ripples spread and multiply and suddenly they are everywhere, the whole landscape undulating at the edge of visibility.

A foot appears inside a ripple. Then a pair of legs, pumping madly. Elsewhere two arms, and two hands balled into fists. An Outsider comes into focus. Then another. In seconds, the murk has become a horde, hundreds of Outsiders running across the sand, sprinting for the widening crack in the gate.

"The gate is opening. All personnel stand clear. The gate is opening." The warning message drones on, echoing through the vast hallways.

There's no other reaction. No one has noticed the incoming horde but us. I hold my breath as they draw close. This is one of my childhood nightmares come to life. One of the things they'd threaten us with to keep us from misbehaving. Be a good boy or the Outsiders will come and get you.

Now they are coming. The gates are wide open for them. And I helped make it possible.

For a moment, terror grips me, bone deep. Maybe I've made a terrible mistake. Maybe Canyon City is fine the way it is. Maybe things can only get worse, not better. Maybe innocent people are about to die for nothing.

Finally, someone else notices them. A lone Guardian starts shooting, blue cannon blasts streaking down through the grey dawn, burning the onrushing Outsiders. An alarm shrieks and another cannon comes to life, then another. Fistfuls of Outsiders are falling now, lying still in the dust. Freedom fighters who will never see their dream of freedom.

But it's too little, too late. The Outsiders are only fifty meters from the gate. Thirty. A woman spins and falls, picked off by the Guardians' cannons. A man's leg is blown off at the knee. Ten meters.

Then they're pouring in through the gap. Ragged, dirty, and angry. Just like the stories always said they'd be. At long last, the Outsider army has come to conquer Canyon City.

Inside the gate, the Guardians are scrambling to form lines, trying to hold back the tide. But most of the Guardians haven't gotten back from the transportation yards yet. The few standing before the gates get overrun like pebbles in a sandstorm.

I gape at the monitors, unable to believe this is really happening. The revolution has truly begun.

"Looks like we missed the party." Ianna enters the room with Spanner. She looks untouched by the battle, and relief surges through me. The Forsaken fulfilled his promise to keep her safe.

I gesture to the chaos outside.

"No, the party is just getting started."

"This was only step two," Shadow says. "Now the real work begins." She looks a little sick. Hopeful, yet stunned by the enormity of what we've done.

I imagine I look sick too.

I make myself focus. Shadow's right, there's no time for dust-dreaming. We've got work to do.

"Grab, do you have a fix on Julius?" I ask.

"He's in his estate, right where we hoped he'd be."

I nod to Shadow and Knott. "Target acquired." I turn to Ianna and Spanner. "Can you hold this room? The Guardians will try to take it back so they can close the gate."

Ianna crosses to the control panel, her eyes sharp. She taps a finger against her lips.

"If I have enough time, I bet I can jam the system so it stays open."

"You will have time." Spanner posts himself inside the doorway, a bristling black sentry. His jaw works as he subvocalizes commands to the other Forsaken.

"You can work that?" I ask.

Ianna quirks an eyebrow at me. "Of course. Why wouldn't I be able to?"

I open my mouth to say something, then simply shake my head. I don't know why I'm surprised. Ianna's sharp as a reaper spine. If anyone has the mind to hack the control panel, she does.

"All right. Be careful." I turn to Shadow and Knott. "We need to let the Outsiders and the Forsaken worry about things in here and down on the ground. The three of us need to do what we came here to do."

They nod, eyes serious and focused. My friends through it all. For a moment I'm overwhelmed with gratitude. I couldn't have done this without them, any of it. Shadow and Knott have had my back from the very beginning. I don't know how I got so lucky. I'm sure I don't deserve it.

Shadow must see some of this in my face.

"Don't go getting all sappy now, Twist. We don't have time for that. Focus."

I snort. "Fine. But if we survive this, I reserve the right to get as sappy as I want."

She grins up at me.

"It's a deal."

42

We slip out onto the wide walkway that runs along the top of the wall. The sun is a warm glow behind the lip of the canyon. Overhead a trio of stars still shine, stubbornly refusing to cede the sky. The air is crisp and cold, making my lips feel brittle. Below, the sounds of battle echo up from the spires of Canyon City. Cannon fire and armor clashing. People screaming and cursing.

We head away from the natural sunrise, toward one of our own making.

The town of Sunrise sits atop the tallest spire in Canyon City, up on the mesa. The elite residents live in the open air and light, while everyone else lives down in the canyon, in the cracks and dust. It sits on the edge of the city, its sheer side facing the scablands. The mesa is so high it forms a natural wall, and the actual city wall runs right into it and stops, before continuing on the far side.

This means we don't have to go to ground level to get to Sunrise: The top of the wall will take us right where we want to go. Which is good, because judging from the sound of the battle, the ground is not a safe place to be right now.

"Do you think the residents are fighting too?" I ask Shadow as we jog along the top of the wall.

"I don't know. Grab's been transmitting the images of the slaughtered Outsiders nonstop, so hopefully they're fighting on our side."

"Grab, what do you see up there?"

Grab's voice comes in through my earcones, so clear he could be standing right next to me. "The residents are mostly staying inside their spires so far. Watching through the windows."

"They are afraid to act," Knott says. "If the revolt fails, they will be punished."

"Well, I hope they make up their minds soon. I don't think we can win this fight without them," I say.

"You don't think your sister and her pet cyborgs can win the war all…" Shadow's voice cuts off as a cannon blast comes out of nowhere, knocking her off her feet.

"Sniper!" Knott yells. "Get down."

She shoves me hard, and the next shot just misses my head. I hear the energy crackling as it burns past my ear.

"Spines! Shadow, are you ok?" I ask.

She doesn't answer, and my heart leaps into my throat. Her covert armor doesn't shrug off damage the way ours does. Have I just lost my best friend?

Then her voice croaks up from behind me. "Yeah, I'm fine."

She doesn't sound fine, though. Her voice is rough and full of pain.

I scan the area for cover. It's slim pickings. The top of the wall was designed so that Guardians patrolling it would have maximum visibility. There's another waist-high wall running along the side, but not much else.

Dust storms. We were hoping the Guardians would be so focused on the fighting down below, nobody would notice a few people moving along the top of the wall.

Apparently, we were wrong.

"Knott, did you get a fix on that sniper's position?"

"They are firing from Sunrise," she says.

"From Sunrise?" I give a low whistle as I raise my head and peer carefully over the edge of the wall. "That's half a kilometer away. Somebody up there is a good shot."

"I don't think you'll be surprised to learn we all know that somebody," Grab says, shifting his drone feed onto my retina display.

The sniper kneels at the edge of the Mesa, cannon balanced atop a tripod. The first rays of the sun melt across their armor like liquid amber. As the camera zooms in on the figure, their face slowly comes into focus.

"Rory." I taste bile, the name bitter in my mouth.

"Everyone's favorite turncoat," Grab agrees. "Returned to stab us in the back again."

"The front," Shadow gasps. She struggles to prop her head and shoulders against the low wall, fingering the scorched hole right below her collarbone. I can see burnt flesh at the bottom, charred black and red. "He shot me in the front."

"That doesn't make it any better." I survey the top of the wall again, hoping to find some better cover. There is none. "We're target practice up here, and it's a long way to Sunrise. It's too far to crawl on our bellies, but the second we stand up, Rory's going to pick us off. Anyone have any suggestions?"

"Perhaps you could fly," Jmini says.

"Now is not the time, Jmini. If you don't have anything useful to say, keep quiet."

"I'm quite serious. Simply leap from the wall. Your gravboots will take you to the ground safely."

"You can't be serious," I say, shuddering. Just the thought makes my throat close up. I may be able to handle them better now, but heights and I will never be friends. "If we jump off the wall, we'll be abandoning our entire plan. The whole point of us being up here is that it's the most direct route to Sunrise and Julius. If we float down to the ground, we'll have to fight our way back up through The Mesa."

"And in case you've forgotten, The Mesa is the Guardians' head-quarters." Shadow chimes in. "The last time we went after Julius through there we got destroyed."

My jaw tightens at the memory of that failed assault. Mai and the Outsiders dying in the dust. Julius out-dueling me beside the under-ground river, then stabbing my dad through the chest when he tried to intervene.

White-hot anger flares in the pit of my stomach. Julius has to pay for what he did.

"Going down is too slow. This is our most direct route. Knott's armor can withstand sniper blasts. So can mine, as long as Rory doesn't hit any weak spots. Shadow, I'm sorry, but we're going to have to leave you here. Grab, tell Ianna to send one of the Forsaken out to carry Shadow back inside."

Shadow's eyes narrow, her mouth setting into a grim line.

"No, Twist. You're not going in there without me." She struggles to get to her feet, grinding her teeth against the pain.

I gently push her back down. "You've done your part, Shadow. You got the gate open. Let us take it from here."

Her eyes shimmer with unshed tears. "Come on, Twist. It's just a flesh wound. I can still fight."

"But can you get across half a kilometer of open wall with Rory taking shots at you? The next blast might hit something more vital, and your armor's not built for that." I crouch in front of her and take her gloved hand in mine. "The last time we went after Julius, I lost my dad. I can't lose you too. We're crew: Everybody has different strengths, different parts of the mission to fulfill. You know that. You've done your part. It's time for us to do ours."

"Fine. Go be the hero." Shadow glares up at me, squeezing my hand tight. "But you'd better not get yourself killed. That goes for you too, Knott. You two are the only family I've got. Swear it, Twist. Swear you'll come back."

I hold her gaze and nod gravely. "I swear. We're not going to leave you, Shadow. We'll be back when this is all over."

They're empty words. I know it, and she knows it too.

Shadow squeezes my hand a final time. "Thank you. May the sun be at your back, Twist."

"May the sun be at your back." I release her gloved hand and turn to Knott. "Are you ready to play shooting-gallery target for half a kilometer?"

She gives me a thumbs up. Her eyes are calm behind her visor. I don't know how she does it. My heart is pounding like a jackhammer.

I take a deep breath and get into a runner's crouch.

"All right, on my mark. Let's go get that spine-sucker."

43

———

Half a kilometer of open wall to cross with the best sniper in Canyon City shooting at us. Whose brilliant idea was this?

Rory's first shot hits me before I've taken four steps, sizzling across my visor like a bolt of lightning. The flash of energy is blinding, the impact snapping my head back like a jab. As I'm reeling, another shot hits me, then a third.

The blasts can't do any real damage from such long distance, but they knock me off balance, making me stumble like a drunk, leaning against the low barrier along the edge of the wall. I get a good look at the sheer drop down the inside of the massive stone barrier. The dusty street waits far below.

Shuddering, I jerk back, cold sweat breaking out across my forehead. Spines, I hate heights.

Rory hits me twice more, knocking me to my knees. I huddle behind the wall, my breath coming in sharp gasps.

"This isn't going to work. He can't penetrate my armor at this distance, but his shots are going to knock me off the wall."

Knott turns to look back at me, her brow crinkled. Rory shifts his aim to her, but he might as well be shooting at the wall itself. His shots have as much effect on her heavy armor as milk blossoms on the wind.

"That's it! Just like in the control room." I bare my teeth in a feral grin. "Knott, get in front of me. Your heavy armor can protect both of us."

Knott dutifully waits while I crawl around behind her and pull myself up off the ground. Rory keeps shooting, but his shots bend away, deflected by the bulk of Knott's armor.

"All right, let's move."

We jog forward at a steady pace. I concentrate on keeping myself in Knott's shadow, giving Rory nothing to shoot at. He keeps a steady stream of energy sizzling into Knott, but it might be grains of sand for all the damage he's doing.

"Rory's cursing up a storm right now," I say.

I can feel Knott's grin. "Yes, he is not very patient."

"You might want to pick up the pace," Grab breaks in. "Reinforcements are on the way. I don't think your little game of peek-a-boo is going to work as well when you've got snipers firing at you from multiple angles."

I groan. "Spines. Why can't anything be easy?"

Grab laughs. "Did you really think assassinating the head of the colony would be easy? You need to recalibrate your difficulty meter, Twist."

We double-time it down the wall. I'm growing warm in my armor, the heat of exertion burning away the morning chill. True to its name, the first rays of the rising sun fall upon the settlement ahead of us. The golden light flashes upon the armor of more snipers setting up in the distance. One of them is dead ahead, directly in my line of sight. I watch them set up their tripod, carefully balancing their cannon. The barrel is like a dead black eye staring straight at me.

All I can do is brace myself. If I try to avoid the sniper, I'll just put myself back into Rory's field of fire.

The first shot hammers my chestplate. I stumble, but manage to stay behind Knott. The follow up hits me in the stomach, huffing my breath out of me.

I'm gasping and sucking air, but still keeping my position behind Knott. The end of the wall is only two hundred meters away.

The next blast hits my knee, kicking my leg out from under me.

Suddenly I'm falling, the hard stone walkway slamming into my shoulder.

Knott jogs ten meters before she realizes I'm no longer beside her. She skids to an uncertain halt. I'm completely exposed.

Cannon fire punches me from at least three directions. I roll against the low barrier, but it does no good. The snipers are spread across the edge of the Sunrise mesa now, and the barrier can't provide cover from all of them.

Knott stands uncertainly in the center of the walkway. She looses a few snapdragon missiles at the snipers, but they're no more than a momentary distraction.

That last two hundred meters might as well be two kilometers.

I lay against the base of the barrier, my mind racing. I'm stuck in no-man's land. Do I try to charge ahead? Do I retreat? If I retreat, the snipers get to shoot at my back, which doesn't sound at all appealing. Jmini's flying idea doesn't sound so bad anymore.

Knott steps back to cover me, exchanging cannon fire with the snipers. I pound the wall in frustration. Nothing ever goes exactly as planned, but I didn't expect our attack to go sideways this soon. Taking out Julius was our fastest road to victory. Now we're stuck. Literally.

A barrage of cannon fire erupts behind me, arcing up over my head, striking at the Sunrise snipers. I turn to see a handful of Forsaken laying down fire, Shadow standing grimly in their midst. Their shots aren't very accurate at such a distance, but they're enough to make the snipers duck and cover.

I grin and raise my fist to Shadow.

She raises her fist back, then pumps it forward. Her message is clear. "Go now, while we've got them pinned down."

You don't have to tell me twice.

I scramble to my feet, head down, arms pumping, Knott lumbering along beside me. If we can get off the wall, we'll be OK. Once we're in Sunrise there will be plenty of cover. Places I can hide and use my greicagin-sight to my advantage.

Sniper fire peppers the wall around us, but they're missing more than they're hitting now. The Forsaken aren't giving them time to aim properly.

We've covered half the distance. Fierce joy pounds through my veins. We're going to make it.

Out of the corner of my eye, I see Rory raise a long tube to his shoulder. My stomach drops. He's going to blow up the whole top of the wall.

The tube puffs smoke and the rocket comes whistling toward us. Even our armor won't save us from that little cone of death.

There are no good choices.

I lurch to the side, burying my shoulder in Knott's side, shoving her toward the edge of the wall with all my strength. The roar of the rocket's explosion hits my ears, heat and dust slamming into me like a wall.

I leap into space.

44

The thing about falling through an explosion is that it's difficult to tell which way is up. Smoke and fire are all around me. Thick dust obscures everything, and a big chunk of rock moving very quickly nearly takes my head off. The force of the explosion tumbles me over and over, like a milkblossom in the wind.

Somewhere, the ground is rushing up at me, but I have no idea which direction that is. This is my worst nightmare, the moment I've been dreading since that day in training when I climbed up the canyon and saw nothing but open sky above me. If I don't figure it out in five seconds, I'll be nothing but a smear on the ground.

Through the smoke and dust, I glimpse the sky, then the wall, then the sky again. I wrestle with my panic. Think! If I know which direction the sky is, the ground should be the other way. I hope.

"Jmini, activate gravboots on my mark." I wait for my next glimpse of blue, praying the smoke hasn't swallowed it up. Time slows, my heart a bass drum in my ears. My visor shows me nothing but smoke and dust and… "Now!"

As my gravboots kick on, a suit of falling armor flashes past the corner of my eye. Knott.

I reach out instinctively. "Maglock!"

My glove attaches itself to her armor with an audible *thunk* ... and her momentum nearly rips my shoulder out of its socket.

I groan. Spines, that armor is heavy.

The whine of my gravboots rises to a scream as they fight to slow both of us down. My shoulders and back are on fire, my arms trembling. The ground is still invisible, but it's got to be close.

Then we hit. My legs piston up into my hips, driving my hips up into my stomach. Meanwhile, my ribs and shoulders continue downward. I'm like a tin can being squashed by the foot of a giant. I try to roll with the momentum, throwing myself forward. It kind of works, and I tumble across the dust like an uprooted lanbrush, rolling over and over.

Finally, I come to rest on my back. Clouds of crimson dust obscure the world around me. I hurt all over.

Still, I'm alive.

"Knott?" I croak.

A low groan is my answer.

"Are you hurt?"

Knott groans again. "A better question is where do I not hurt?"

"Roger that." I laugh weakly and gaze up at the smooth face of the wall. It seems even bigger when you're lying on the ground next to it.

I peel myself up and find Knott lying nearby. I offer her a hand.

"I guess we're even now."

"Even?" She groans as I pull her to her feet.

"Remember when you carried me down that cliff during training? Now I've carried you too."

Knott chuckles. "Even. Yes, I say we are even."

She turns, taking in the debris surrounding us. A good section of wall has fallen with us, and the street running along the base of the wall is clogged with broken rocks, some of them as big as a gravbike. We're lucky we didn't get squashed flat.

"So," Knott says. "What do we do now?"

A hundred meters down the street rises the base of the Mesa. I follow the towering spire with my eyes, all the way up to where Sunrise gleams atop its plateau. Julius sits upon his throne there, lording over Canyon City like some monstrous tick, growing fat off the blood of the workers.

We were so close. Just a couple of hundred meters away. Now…

I sigh. "I guess we'll have to take the long way."

Before I can take a step, an armored Guardian steps out of the Mesa. Then another. In seconds their number has grown to ten, with more on the way.

A chill slides down my spine. Did I really think we could waltz right into the Mesa? Take the lift straight up to Sunrise? My plan has fallen apart before it could even get started.

I go to shoulder my cannon and realize I've lost it somewhere in the fall. So I draw my warpknife instead. Beside me, Knott gives me a nod and draws hers as well. If we go down, we go down fighting.

The Guardians form up into neat lines, two dozen cannons leveled at us. They advance in precise lockstep.

I always thought my last stand would be more glamorous than this. When I was a kid, I dreamed of going down while heroically saving someone from a Rock Horror. More recently, I figured it would be Julius who did the job. Not being cut down in the street by anonymous Guardians.

I suppose this way is fitting. I started as a nobody down here in the dust. It's right that I should end this way too.

Knott and I are good, but there's no way we can fight so many at once. We'll be overwhelmed by sheer numbers.

There's no question of capture. Julius has made it clear he prefers us dead. The Guardians spread out, moving to surround us. Coming in for the kill.

I crouch, letting my blind eye take over, shifting into my greicagin-sight. The Guardians' power blurs one into the next, the whole group shining like a red star. A star coming to burn me to a crisp. All I can do is take as many of them with me as possible.

I look into faces as hard as granite. There's no question of friend-ship now. No former friends or classmates. This is all business. And the business is murder.

As I prepare to meet their attack, a distant roaring reaches my ears. I cock my head, listening. The roar comes from everywhere, reverberating off the walls and spires of Canyon City, building and getting louder. Like a flash flood rushing down a canyon.

The Guardians look around, trying to figure out where the sound is coming from.

The roar has transformed into a rising and falling wave of sound. There are voices within it, shouting and chanting.

A crowd of people surges into view, flooding around a spire behind me. Hundreds of them, filling the street. As I watch, more surge in from every direction. They're brandishing clubs and knives. Rusty lengths of metal.

Their voices are cursing and angry. Releasing years of bottled-up rage.

Underneath the roar, I notice a repeated word, chanted by dozens of lips. It grows louder as more voices take it up.

It takes me a moment to figure out what they're saying. Then the word become clear.

"Cyclops! Cyclops!"

My mouth drops open. They're chanting my name.

45

Voices rise as the crowd sees the Guardians. Angry insults are flung, weapons brandished. The Guardians' eyes are wide behind their visors. They grip their cannons tight, struggling to understand what's happening. They step back in twos and threes, trying to keep their distance from the crowd.

The mob moves forward, hesitantly at first, then with increasing confidence as the Guardians retreat. Jeers and insults echo off the wall. I see at least a dozen of Zetta's thumpers out there at the front, broad-shouldered toughs facing the Guardians with their nail-studded clubs and rusty lengths of pipe. It looks like Zetta's decided to honor our agreement.

A woman in the crowd notices my face. Her mouth falls open, finger stretching out in my direction.

"Cyclops!"

More protestors take up the cry. In seconds, I'm surrounded by the dirty faces of miners. All shouting this new name they've given me.

The people crowd around me, reaching out their hands, trying to touch me like I'm some kind of magic totem. They press close, overwhelming me with the warmth of their bodies, the scent of their breath and sweat.

Knott gives a cry of surprise and wraps her arms around a teenage boy. As they break their embrace, I see he's got her black hair and wide, flat face. She turns to me with a smile.

"Twist, this is my little brother, Sami."

"Little" isn't a word I'd use to describe the boy. Even at his age, he's taller than most people I know, though he doesn't quite have Knott's bulk yet. Still, he's a big boy.

He shakes my hand, smiling shyly.

"It's nice to finally meet you," I say. "I've heard a lot about you."

Sami blushes at that, and studies the ground around his feet. I laugh, remembering what it was like to be that young and self-conscious.

Other people press forward, wanting to speak to me, to shake my hand. The lined faces of mothers and fathers. Dirty, exhausted children. These are the people I grew up with.

There's something different about them today. Something in their eyes. For the first time in my life, these people don't look beaten and bitter. There's more than just anger in their faces. There's hope too, shining like the pole star.

"Cyclops! Cyclops!" They grin and cheer, stretching out their hands to me like I'm some kind of messiah.

I grin back; their joy is infectious. A minute ago, I was prepared to die. Now I'm ready to live.

"Speech! Speech!" They guide me to a boulder, helping me up onto the top of the rock.

I stand there, staring out at a sea of hopeful faces. The Guardians huddle at the base of the Mesa, pressed back by the swelling throng. I see Zetta standing among her thumpers at the edge of the crowd, facing the Guardians down. She catches my eye and nods. I return the nod, stunned. When I was a street kid, Zetta was one of my worst nightmares. I was terrified she'd catch me raiding her scrapyards and cut my fingers off. Now we're on the same side. Strange times make for strange allies.

Knott stands beside Sami. She's smiling, but her brow is creased. She's unsure what to make of all this. That's fair. I don't know what to make of it either.

My stomach flutters. My fingers and toes tingle as if I'm standing on the edge of a cliff. Standing here, being looked up to by hundreds of people is one of the strangest experiences of my life. Excitement and terror war within me. Dread and anticipation.

It's like the first time I stood on top of the Sunrise mesa. Up out of the canyons, with the whole sky spread out above me. Blue stretching forever, limitless, unbound by the earthen walls I'd spent my whole life within.

Then, it was too much. Too much sky, too much sunshine, too much freedom. I wasn't ready for it.

Now, looking at hundreds of faces streaked with crimson dust, I realize I am ready. Ready to throw off the chains that have held me down my whole life. Ready to leave the walls behind. Ready to be free.

The crowd quiets as I open my mouth. Jmini triggers the speakers built into my armor, and my amplified voice booms over the square.

"People of Canyon City! Today is the day you've been waiting for."

A cheer rises from the crowd, and I realize how true my words are. They have been waiting for this day. Waiting their whole lives.

"For generations the IEC has lied to us, used us as indentured servants. They've dangled the carrot of freedom before us, always keeping it just beyond our outstretched fingers."

Every eye in the crowd is on me, their faces rapt with attention. Hanging on my every word. For a moment my sight shifts back to my blind eye, and I see the dust sparkling on their skins. The dust they live and work in, ground into their skins so deep they can never wash it off.

That crimson dust transforms them into a sea of red power, making them burn and shift. A steady stream of people flows in from every direction, swelling the crowd bigger and bigger. The Guardians are gathering too, clustered around the edges, but they seem small and insignificant beside the enormous crowd. I ignore them. Together these people are brighter than any Guardian.

"Today we are done with carrots. The Sunrisers are not us. They live up there, in a world of light and air, while we live down in the dust and shadow. For three generations they have lied to us, growing rich off our sweat. Turning our sisters and brothers into slaves.

Working our fathers and mothers until their hands are ground down to the bone. Yoking us to the same lies, so that we can take their places and continue the cycle, red dust and red blood mixing over and over and over.

"Where will it end? How much blood is enough? The answer is: It will never be enough. The IEC are vampires, sucking this planet dry. And they will keep doing it as long as we allow them to."

The crowd is hushed, hanging on my every word. Their blood sparkles and surges, swirling like wind through the spires. My own heart swells in time, pounding in my ears. I wish I could reach out and touch all of them. Wrap my arms around them and squeeze. They are me, and I am them, and we are all Greica. We are all crimson dust.

I take a deep breath and raise my warpknife. "No more! That all ends today. They will suck us dry no longer. Today we fight back. Today we take this city, and this planet. Today we take what is ours!"

The answering roar of the crowd shakes my bones. Every hand is raised, every fist clenched in defiance. The sound shakes the wall, shakes the spires of Canyon City. It swells and grows, building and echoing. The sound fills me, fills all of Canyon City. It's bigger than me. Bigger than the people standing here. If we get enough voices we can shake Greica, shake the entire planet down to its foundations.

That's when the Guardians attack.

46

The first shot hits me in the chest, knocking me back. I stumble over the surface of the boulder, my foot coming down on air. Suddenly I'm falling.

The wind huffs out of me as my back hits the ground. Screams fill the air. Shouts of anger and pain replace the echoing defiance of moments ago.

The Guardians are attacking.

I curse at my own foolishness. I saw them gathering around the edges of the crowd, yet I ignored them. I let myself get caught up in the moment. With so many people watching me, hanging on my every word, I felt like we had already won. I felt invincible.

Spine-sucking idiot.

Rolling to my feet, I try to assess the situation. The crowd is surging around me, a roiling mass of chaos. I can't see a thing beyond the first ranks.

I scramble back up onto the boulder, throwing myself flat on the top. At the edge of the crowd, lines of Guardians with shields are holding Zetta's thumpers back. Behind them, more Guardians stand with cannons, blasting away at the protestors. People fall like sand in a storm.

I know the Guardians are only stunning people, but it's still shocking to watch so many fall so quickly. At least I hope they're only stunning people. The alternative is too vile to consider.

The thumpers are clubbing at the Guardians' helmets with their metal bars and lengths of wood. I watch a Guardian go down beneath their onslaught. And another. Other protestors take heart from these victories and surge to join the attack.

The protestors' victories are too few, though, and the Guardians' armor is too tough. Most of their blows simply bounce off, and all the attacker gets is a face full of cannon for his trouble. For every Guardian that goes down, dozens of protestors are blasted into submission.

This is a disaster. The protestors aren't soldiers. Their enthusiasm and willingness to fight are no match for superior training and equipment.

Knott wades through the battle in her black armor, smashing down Guardians like the Tank she is, but she's only one person.

My mind spins, trying to come up with a plan. A way to turn the battle. I consider and discard ideas in rapid succession, each one feeling more useless than the last. The optimism and hope I felt moments ago is gone, replaced by panic and dread.

"Grab! We need help down here!"

"I'm on it. Spanner's sending some Forsaken your way, but it's going to take a few minutes."

I curse, surveying the slaughter before me. We don't have a few minutes. In a few minutes, this battle will be over.

We need something big. Something to turn the tide.

Then I spot him. Something big indeed.

Ghengis stands at the foot of the Mesa, face stretched in a sadistic grin as he hacks down protestors. The edge of his warpknife burns red, not the green of safemode, and it's stained with blood the same color. He's killing people, and he's enjoying it.

I stand up and scream. "Ghengis!"

My amplified voice carries over the crowd. He looks up and sees me. His grin grows wider, and he deliberately cuts down another protestor, holding my gaze as the tip of his warpknife emerges from the man's back.

Rage burns through me as I leap off the boulder. My only thought is to stop Ghengis. I may not be able to win the entire battle by myself, but at least I can keep that spine-sucking sadist from killing anyone else.

A howl of pure pain brings me up short.

Knott has her head back, keening with grief and fury. Her face is a dark mask, her eyes locked on the body in Ghengis's hands. My mouth goes dry as I recognize the black hair and oval face of Sami. His lifeless eyes stare back at me. Minutes ago he was shaking my hand, his palm warm against mine, smiling and shy. Now he's dead.

I step toward Ghengis, but Knott shoulders me aside with a snarl. "He is mine."

Ghengis's smile slips a notch as he sees the look on Knott's face. It feels like the entire battle holds its breath as the two giants close in on one another. Their warpknives collide with a sound like a thunderclap.

Ghengis is bigger and stronger, but not by much. Knott can out-muscle any two normal men put together, and her rage and grief lend extra force to her blows. She knocks Ghengis back, pushing him out of the crowd, until it's just the two of them standing in the clear. Two titans going toe-to-toe.

I want to help Knott, but this is her battle. She asked for it, and she deserves the chance to extract her own vengeance. Besides, she can take care of herself. There are plenty of people here who can't say the same.

I leave her to it and dash around the square, fighting where I must and helping where I can. The battle dissolves into a series of sharp vignettes—spraying a bandage on a protestor's wound here, slicing through a Guardian's armor there. The world returns to stop-motion, with no time to plan or anticipate the next movement. I'm caught in the crowd, in the chaos, and all I can do is see and react, again and again in a series of binary choices: move backward or forward, parry or attack, heal or kill.

Despite my best efforts, I can feel us losing momentum. I catch a glimpse of Zetta, hard-pressed and bleeding from a dozen wounds. It looks like she's only got a handful of thumpers left. The Guardians move forward step by step, tightening the cage around us. Every time I cut one down, two more take their place. We're hemmed in with nowhere to run.

My back presses against cold stone, the boulder where I stood only minutes ago, full of hope, giving a speech about freedom. Now I'm hemmed in by three Guardians, and everywhere I look people are bleeding and dying around me.

Desperation rises within me, panic searing the back of my throat. This isn't the way this was supposed to go. Our revolution is stillborn.

I hope Knott got her revenge at least. I haven't seen her or Ghengis since she pushed him out of the crowd. I hope wherever she is, she's doing better than I am.

Because I'm not doing well at all.

My greicagin-sight lets me stay ahead of my attackers, but just barely. There are three of them spread out in a semi-circle around me, coming at me from all sides. I'm parrying and dodging blows like a whirlwind, but it's taking all my skill and speed just to defend. I have no hope of launching a counterattack.

Then a fourth Guardian joins the ring. And a fifth. Forget counter-attacking—I think my chances of staying alive just went out the window.

I snarl and prepare for one last, desperate attack. If I'm going down, I'm going to take as many of them with me as I can.

Before I can lunge forward, a new sound reaches my ears. Screams and a rising wave of panic.

At the edge of the crowd, a sight I never expected. The stuff of my childhood nightmares, brought to life in the light of day.

A Rock Horror as big as a house rears up, tearing into the ring of Guardians, its pincers shredding silver armor like smoke. Another moves in beside it, and another.

A rider in antique armor sits atop the lead Hubzoh, his warpknife hacking down left and right. A legend from the past, resurrected to save the present. A rusty blade, shining once again.

47

Rust salutes me above the crowd. I raise my warpknife in return, hope rekindling in my breast. The Hubzoh have come to fight beside us.

The Guardians react instinctively, their training taking over. They forget about the protestors, scrambling to face this new threat. A ring of silver armor forms, a long arc keeping the Hubzoh from moving deeper into the city.

I goggle at the giants, staring with open-mouthed astonishment at Rust, riding Akona like some cavalry general from old Earth. How did he get so many of them inside the wall? I doubt they came in through the front gate. Though I guess if we were able to sneak in through Zetta's cellar, the Hubzoh probably could too. Or some other cellar. This is their planet, after all. They probably know more secret tunnels than we've ever uncovered, even after a hundred years of digging.

The Hubzoh lash out, their crystalline pincers tearing through armor like it isn't there. It's horrifying. Seeing so many of the Horrors together triggers all my childhood fears. I want to run screaming and never look back. I have to keep reminding myself that these are our allies. They're on our side now.

With an effort, I tear my eyes away from the conflict. This distraction is an opportunity. I can't afford to waste it.

The protestors are frozen, staring at the Hubzoh, terror in their eyes. They're half a second away from breaking, running back to the safety of their homes.

I can't let that happen.

"People of Canyon City!" I leap back onto my boulder, using my armor to amplify my voice again. "Do not be afraid! The Hubzoh are not the monsters we've been told they are. They are intelligent creatures, and this is their home. If invaders came into your home and started killing your family, wouldn't you fight back?"

Eyes turn to look at me, their fear held at bay by the thinnest of margins. They're listening, but their instincts are still screaming at them to run.

"The IEC lied to us about the Hubzoh. In order to get the mining permits they needed, the scientists of the first expedition couldn't let anyone know the Hubzoh were intelligent. So they covered up their findings. They called them "Horrors" and convinced us they were mindless killing machines. They launched a war to exterminate them."

The people are listening now. IEC abuses are easy to believe. We've been suffering them for generations.

"Now is our chance." I point to the battle lines. "We have allies who can fight the Guardians on even ground. If we add our strength to theirs, we can take back Canyon City. Take back this planet. Take back our lives. But we must act now. Hit the Guardians while they're distracted. Who is with me?"

For a moment, stunned silence is my only answer. The people stare, first at me, then at the line of Guardians, and the giant Hubzoh challenging them. I can practically hear them trying to change the path of their thinking, to unlearn truths they've known their whole lives. It's a difficult thing to do, and as I stand there, alone above the crowd, I don't know if they're going to make it. Their ingrained fear of the Hubzoh might be too strong, the memory of their recent beating at the hands of the Guardians too fresh. The entire revolution balances on a the edge of a warpknife.

Then a voice rings out.

"I am with you."

I look up to find Knott standing at the edge of the crowd, her bloody warpknife held high. Her black armor is sliced to pieces, torn away entirely in patches, exposing patches of flesh beneath. But her eyes are steady, her mouth a line of resolve.

Relief blows through me. She's alive. She beat Ghengis.

Then another voice calls out.

"I too."

"And I."

The wind blows through the crowd, lifting voices. In moments, the square is caught up in a storm of enthusiasm.

"There." I point again at the Guardians. Their backs are to us, their attention fixed on the half dozen Hubzoh towering over them. "There is your enemy."

With a roar, the crowd surges forward, rusty pipes clubbing down upon the unprepared Guardians. Caught between two foes, the Guardians' lines begin to crumble.

I call out through my com. "Knott, I need you to lead here. Keep the people focused. Work together with Rust to fight the Guardians down here on the ground."

"And where will you be?" Her tone of voice tells me she already suspects the answer.

"I'm going after Julius. It's time to put an end to this."

48

The Guardians are caught between the protestors and the Hubzoh, leaving the entrance to the Mesa undefended. I slip in past the fountain, breathing in the moist air, and remember the first time I ever passed through these doors. The day I came for the Guardian Tournament. I was struck by how clean everything was, and how incredible that they had enough water for a fountain. All I wanted then was to find my sister, and I thought becoming a Guardian would give me the power to do it.

It turns out I was right. Becoming a Guardian did give me the resources to find Ianna. But I never imagined all the other things that would come along with that. My dad being alive, and then dead again. The Outsiders. The Hubzoh. The lies and greed of the IEC. The slavers and corruption at the very top of Canyon City, lead by Julius Carlyle.

It's all wrong. And it all stops today.

I slip through the changing room, past the rows of cubbies where I had to abandon all the possessions of my former life. In here, I pulled on the loose, one-size-fits-all brown clothing of a novice.

Next, I step out into the cavern where I met Shadow and Kass, and all the other members of my training class. The place where Castle's projected face announced that half of us wouldn't graduate the program. That our struggle was just beginning.

A small smile curls my lips as I picture Shadow punching Ghengis in the jewels here, sparking an all-out brawl between Rockheads and Sunrisers. The smile withers and dies as I remember that Ghengis is probably dead now. Like Octav and my dad and Mai and so many others.

The entire Mesa reeks of death. All of Canyon City does. All of Greica.

I let my greicagin-sight take over as I move into the tunnels, the labyrinth we raced through on that first day, pitted against each other in a race to get inside Merrimack. Eager to discover our team assignments.

Now the tunnels are cold and silent. Dark except for the faint red glow of the greicagin dust embedded in the walls.

There are easier ways to get inside the Mesa. I could have taken the lift, or walked in the front door. But those ways will be watched. In all the chaos, I'm hoping they've forgotten about this one.

It's strange navigating this labyrinth alone. Last time I was here, it was full of the other novices, jostling and racing for position. Rory walked beside me, bleeding from a nasty wound on his scalp.

At the thought of Rory, my grip tightens on the hilt of my warp-knife. Even after all this time, I still can't believe he betrayed us in our final game. He sold out his own crew to Ghengis. I know you've got to look out for yourself, but I'll never understand what could drive someone to stoop that low.

Jmini interrupts my thoughts. "Quit gathering dust, Twist. I'm detecting movement ahead."

I freeze, snapping my focus back to the present. Sure enough, there are little knots of power moving through the labyrinth. Guardians.

"Do you think they've seen me?" I subvocalize carefully.

"I don't believe so. Their movements suggest a search pattern. I'd say they suspect you're in here, but they're still trying to pin down exactly where."

"Good. Let's keep it that way."

I slip forward as quietly as I can, carefully placing each foot on the dust. I watch the Guardians through my blind eye. Their greicagin-powered implants make them shine like little red stars moving in the darkness. The walls of the labyrinth glow more faintly, disappearing entirely in some places as the concentration of greicagin dust within them fluctuates. It's strange, like looking at a spotty, incomplete map within the Game. I have to fight the urge to curse at my Mapper.

"Do you think we can avoid them?" I whisper.

"Doubtful. There are a limited number of exits from the labyrinth. It wouldn't be terribly difficult to cover all of them."

"Well, I guess as long as surprise is still on our side, we'd better use it," I say.

I focus on the glowing form closest to me. The Guardian is three turns away in the labyrinth, maybe fifty meters moving in a straight line. I tiptoe up to an intersection and press myself against the wall. Then I palm a disruptor mine and wait.

"You know we don't have many disruptors left." Jmini says. "Your warpknife would be every bit as effective."

"My warpknife would kill them, Jmini. I'm tired of killing people. These Guardians are just grunts doing their job, they don't deserve to die for it. If I can take them out without killing them, I will."

"A commendable goal. I just hope you don't need your disruptor mines later."

"Me too, Jmini. But I'm not going to kill someone to save mines for later. Now be quiet, they're almost here."

The Guardian approaches down the passage to my left. They're moving fast, probably thinking only of getting the job done quickly and getting home. After all, they're only hunting one person, and they've got plenty of backup. What could they possibly have to worry about?

As they step into the intersection, I answer that question for them, stepping forward and slapping the disruptor mine to their chestplate in one smooth motion. Their armor locks up, and topple without a sound.

"One down."

I drag them out of the intersection and prop them against the wall in the dark. Hopefully their crew will find them later.

There are three more Guardians between me and the end of the labyrinth, and I deal with them each of them in a similar fashion.

"That was the last of your disruptor mines," Jmini laments, as I drag the final immobilized Guardian out of the way.

"Yup." I draw my warpknife from its sheath, the greicagin-powered blade blazing in the darkness. "Looks like I've saved all the lives I can."

"I hope you do not regret your decision."

"Saving lives is always the right decision, Jmini. That's the reason for this revolution. The IEC doesn't value lives, they only value profit. It's about people, Jmini. People and Hubzoh and Forsaken and whatever other forms of life we encounter out there. Life is the most valuable thing there is."

"The time of life is short; To spend that shortness basely were too long."

I smile. "Yeah, something like that."

As I approach the end of the labyrinth, the complex beyond blazes in my greicagin-sight. The interior of the Mesa hums with power, making it almost impossible to differentiate objects. The entire space flares like the sun.

I release my greicagin-sight with a sigh.

"It looks like it's just you and me and my plain old eyeball for this part, Jmini."

"Don't worry, Twist. You and me and your eyeball will do just fine."

I'm not convinced, but I appreciate the vote of confidence.

The rough walls of the labyrinth give way to the smooth interior of the Mesa. I step out into a broad hallway, my boots ringing on the polished stone tiles.

A dozen Guardians block the hall in either direction, cannons and warpknives pointed right at me.

Kass flashes me her perfect smile.

"Glad you could join us, Twist. We've been expecting you."

49

I eye the Guardians surrounding me. There's six on each side, neatly closing the trap. Too many to fight at once. I focus on their leader instead.

"Kass. It's not too late, you know. You can still be on the right side of history here."

Kass's musical laugh tugs at my heart.

"The right side of history? Your revolution is history, Twist. Did you really think a bunch of Outsiders could defeat the Guardians? You really are a rockhead. Take his warpknife and secure him."

I try to fight, but it's hopeless. There's too many of them. In short order they've disarmed me and slapped magcuffs around my wrists, locking my arms behind my back.

They haul me to my feet like a sack of mine dust. I stare at Kass, shaking with helpless rage. It wasn't supposed to end like this.

"I thought we had something special," I say softly. "But you're just like all the rest of them, aren't you?"

She flinches, but her blue eyes don't waver.

"I never pretended to be anything else, Twist. Your optimism has always been your weakness. You saw what you wanted to see."

Her crew hauls me away, taking me deeper into the heart of the Mesa.

"Jmini, contact Grab. Find out what's going on outside."

There's silence for a few seconds before Jmini answers. When he does, his voice is uncharacteristically hesitant.

"I'm not getting any response from Grab. I'm afraid the Guardians might have discovered what he was doing."

My breath catches in my throat. Grab is paralyzed and blind, tied to a life-support system in a hospital bed. His network was his only contact. If they've cut his mind off from that…

I grind my teeth. At best Grab is alone in the dark, cut off from the world; at worst he could be injured or dead.

Shadow is shot, Grab is missing in action, and I've gotten myself captured. Not the most efficient way to run a revolution.

Three of Kass's men lead me to a lift and load me inside. Kass stands at the front of the lift, staring at the wall.

"You can't even look at me, can you?" I ask.

She doesn't turn her head. "I've seen enough."

"I thought you were different, Kass. I thought you cared about right and wrong."

"I do care about right and wrong. That's why I'm a Guardian."

I laugh. "Guardians don't care about right and wrong. Guardians are mercenaries waiting to cash their next paycheck."

Kass turns to face me, her face cold as an exposed cliff.

"My father was a Guardian. My grandfather too. My family has protected this colony since it was built."

"Protected it from what? From the people in Canyon City? The people who spend their sweat and blood down in the mines?"

"From the Horrors. Or did you forget about the killing machines that are native to this planet? Without the Guardians, the Horrors would have torn this colony apart."

I shake my head and smile sadly.

"That's the story the IEC has always sold us, and you've swallowed it whole. The Horrors' real name is Hubzoh. The IEC called them Horrors because it sounds scary, and humans always want to exterminate scary things. They're intelligent, did you know that? I've communicated with them."

"If they're so intelligent why are they always throwing themselves at our walls? Doesn't seem very intelligent to me."

"They attack us because we attack them. We launched a genocidal campaign against them and called it a war."

"That's ridiculous. They attacked us and we attacked them. That's a war."

"Of course the IEC call it a war, Kass. It's hard to rally public opinion around genocide. It's easy to convince people to get behind a war."

Kass shakes her head. "Your theory is ridiculous. If the Horrors were intelligent, we wouldn't even be on this planet."

"Exactly. If the Horrors were intelligent, the colony wouldn't have been approved, and the IEC wouldn't be able to mine greicagins. But if they label the Hubzoh as mindless monsters who are trying to kill us? That's a picture simple enough for anyone to understand."

Kass looks at me for a long moment, then sighs and turns away. "I feel sorry for you, Twist. Someone has been filling your head with milkweed. You don't even know which way is up anymore."

The lift slides to a halt and the doors iris open. They push me out into a garden, red and white blooms beneath a clear blue sky. The wind whistles in from the horizon, smelling crisp and clean, making the stalks nod as if they're agreeing with some invisible speaker. A familiar white manor house looms over everything.

50

"The Carlyle estate." I curl my lip into a sneer. "You're not even pretending the Guardians are in charge anymore, are you?"

"The Guardians were never in charge, Twist." Julius comes strolling out of the house, Rory and Castle right behind him. His white suit is spotless and he's holding a drink in one hand. There are people fighting and dying below, and he looks like he hasn't got a care in the world. "You know that."

I stand up straight and look him in the eye. "Julius. Imagine my complete lack of surprise."

"Well, I am the governor of this colony. Who would you expect to serve up justice? Castle?" He laughs. "Castle's kind of like a cannon: Good for hitting targets once you aim him, but without a guiding hand he's useless."

Castle's lips curl into a scowl, but he remains silent. I'm impressed. I didn't think anything could keep Castle's mouth shut.

Julius strolls closer, red flowers brushing against the white legs of his pants. The curved sheath of his warpknife hangs from his belt like a question mark. He takes a sip of his drink, some kind of orange cocktail with green leaves on top.

"You know, I should thank you, Twist. If you hadn't eliminated me from that qualifying run, I would have become a Guardian. Another mindless tool in the hands of the powerful. Like Castle here, nothing more than a warpknife, cutting whatever I was pointed at.

"But you derailed all that. You forced me to find a different path, a better path. And now…" He lifts his eyebrows, and spreads his arms wide. "I am governor of the entire colony. King of all I survey. And I owe it all to you."

"You killed my dad," I growl.

"And you killed my brother," he snaps back, his mouth pressing into a thin line, grey eyes going hard. "Blood for blood. I'd say that makes us even."

"What about my sister and the other slaves? What about the things you did to them?"

He brushes this away with a flick of his fingers.

"You mean my household slaves? You'll never prove it. If you ask them, the men and woman at my estate will tell you they work here voluntarily. If there were any slaves in this colony, that would be a problem. Fortunately, there are not."

"Just like there isn't intelligent life on this planet?"

"Precisely. There is none because I say there is none. I'm glad we understand each other, Twist." Julius smiles and draws his warpknife. The blade hums softly, a glowing arc of red in my greicagin sight. He levels the point at my heart. "Now, do you have any last words before you die?"

"Yes. Shadow, did you get all that?"

Shadow's voice comes from a tiny drone circling overhead.

"Loud and clear, Twist. I'm streaming it out live to all of Canyon City."

Julius's smile wavers, then he clamps it back onto his face.

"Public opinion? You think you're going to win this fight with public opinion? You have a lot to learn. I'm sorry you have to die in ignorance."

He lunges forward, driving his warpknife toward the center my chest. My death is in his eyes.

Kass kicks me in the side, tumbling me to the ground. Julius's warpknife hisses past my ear.

"We don't allow cold-blooded executions of prisoners, Governor." Kass steps in front of me. "If Twist is guilty, he needs to go to trial like anyone else."

Julius rounds on her, snarling. "I make the laws here. And I say he dies now."

"In that case, he's entitled to a trial by combat."

My manacles click open as Kass tosses me my warpknife. The familiar weight settles into my palm. The blade hums to life.

She nods to me. "You're on your own now."

I nod back, wondering at her sudden change of heart. Was this her plan all along? To get me close to Julius? By arresting me and bringing me to him, was she actually trying to help me?

"Thanks, Kass. It's good to see some Guardians still respect the law."

I rise and face Julius. His face is twisted with rage.

"Fine, you can have your little trial. Don't expect it to work out any better than it did the last time we dueled. Maybe I'll take your other eye this time, then cut you apart piece by piece." He smiles. "Yes, I think that's exactly what I'll do."

As he mentions my eye, hot anger flashes through me. The last time we crossed blades, he toyed with me. He laughed as he took my eye and he took my dad.

Not this time.

Cold resolve replaces the anger as I shift my attention to that same blind eye. He may have taken my eye, but he inadvertently gave me something else. Something that's going to help me bring him down once and for all.

The world turns red, as my greicagin sight flows in.

51

Julius smiles, lifting his blade high in the scorpion-tail dueling style the Carlyle brothers favor. He probes my defenses with quick, darting thrusts, his movements easy and relaxed. One, two, three. He's not worried at all. It never even crosses his mind that he might lose this duel.

And with good reason. Julius has been training with the warpknife his entire life. He and his brother were two of the best duelists I've ever seen. Every time I've fought them, they've defeated me easily, penetrating my defenses as if they didn't exist.

But I've been training with the greatest general Canyon City's ever seen. This time, I'm prepared.

I grit my teeth and crouch low, focusing all my attention through my blind eye. Julius becomes a being of pure power, flaring with each movement.

He keeps lunging in from my blind side, trying to take advantage of my weakness, forcing me to circle. He thrusts and I parry, but his strikes are getting closer. I'm barely staying ahead of his probing blade.

I try to anticipate his movements by focusing on the greicagin-power shifting within him. But there's something wrong with his form.

He's not glowing bright like Rust or the other Guardians I've fought. Julius is only a faint outline, like the walls of the labyrinth below.

Then it hits me. Julius isn't a Guardian. He doesn't have a shard implanted in his collar bone. I can't see the power shifting within him the way I can with Rust or the others.

Ice slides down my spine. If I can't use my greicagin-sight to anticipate his movements, I'm in trouble.

Suddenly I'm thinking too much; the same problem I always had in Merrimac. My parries become jerky and a beat too slow. Julius cuts a hot line down my left forearm, then slashes me across the thigh. Blood slicks the inside of my armor.

His smile widens, and he becomes even more relaxed. Now that I'm injured, time is on his side. He can toy with me, drawing out the duel while blood loss makes me weaker and weaker.

I focus harder, trying to see the greicagin dust powdering his skin and clothes. But Julius isn't a grubby rockhead like me. His skin is clean, his white suit sparkling. There's not much dust on him at all.

Besides, what good does seeing the dust on his skin do me? It doesn't flare before he moves, like the shard-powered implants inside the Guardians. It only tells me where he is, and I can see that just fine with my regular eye.

Julius attacks again, thrusting toward my stomach, then changing targets at the last second, flicking the tip of his warpknife up toward my good eye. I barely flinch out of the way, and receive a scratch across my forehead instead.

His grin becomes malicious. He really is trying to take out my other eye. Blind me, so he can cut me apart piece by piece.

Blood from the fresh cut trickles down over my eyebrow, and I have to wipe it away with the back of my hand. Wonderful. If Julius's warpknife doesn't blind me, my own blood is going to do the job.

I shuffle backward, alternately parrying Julius's thrusts and wiping away blood. Then Julius launches a sustained flurry of blows, and I don't have time to wipe blood anymore. I parry furiously, my warpknife a blur, all of the reflexes I've honed in my training sessions with Rust pushed to their limits. If it weren't for those sessions, I'd be dead already. Even with my new skills, it's all I can do to stay alive.

Julius scratches my shoulder, then my ribs. He lands a shallow slash across my stomach, drawing blood again. I can feel myself slowing down, growing tired as the blood loss takes its toll. The muscles in my knife-arm are heavy as stones.

Then the trickle of blood gets in my eye. A wash of tears springs up, blurring the world around me. I wipe at the blood with the back of my hand, frantically trying to blink the tears away, but it feels like all I do is smear the salty blood into my eye more. My eye flares with pain and squeezes shut involuntarily. The world goes black.

Julius's mocking voice comes from my left. "Oh, would you look at that?" I feel the sting of his blade penetrating my shoulder. I slash out wildly in that direction, slicing only air. Julius laughs. "Aw, that's too bad. You can't look, can you?"

Panic closes my throat. I'm blind. Utterly helpless.

My heartbeat thunders in my ears, my breath clawing to get out. I'm at Julius's mercy. I'm going to die here.

Despair smothers me. I've failed. I've let Ianna down. I'm never going to avenge our dad.

Julius sinks his blade into one thigh and then the other. My legs collapse, leaving me kneeling in the dust. I put all my focus into my greicagin-sight, and manage to zero in on his faint dust-outline, circling around me. But what's the point of seeing him coming now? It's too late for it to make any difference. I'm already on my knees and bleeding from half a dozen wounds. Even if I can see him coming, there's no way I can defend myself like this.

I look beyond him, at the bright shapes of the Guardians standing in a wide circle around us. I hope Julius doesn't punish Kass for freeing me. She took a big chance granting me this trial by combat. Maybe she still cares, after all. I'm sorry I couldn't reward her faith in me.

Julius is circling me, strutting and monologuing like some cartoon villain. I tune him out. I'm not going to spend the last moments of my life listening to that spine sucker.

My focus wanders over the other Guardians. Rory's got his cannon pointed straight at me. I don't take it personally, that's just the way Rory is. Always ready to shoot something. The power flowing through

Rory's cannon gathers into a bright star, flaring behind the on/off switch that toggles when someone presses the firing stud.

A familiar sadness fills me as I look at Rory. I still don't know what went wrong between us. What I could have done differently, or better. How could he have been so unhappy that he betrayed our crew to Ghengis? As long as I live, I'll never understand it.

Of course, that won't be long now, will it?

The faint shape of Julius passes between us, his monologue winding down. Soon he'll get tired of talking. He'll run his warpknife through my heart and that will be that.

My gaze wanders back to Rory, something about him tickling the back of my brain. I stare at his glowing outline, at the cannon pointed right at my face.

Then it hits me.

Julius is behind me, still circling. I shift on my knees so that I'm facing directly toward Rory's cannon. Now I need to get Julius back in front of me.

"You love to listen to yourself talk, Julius," I say, interrupting his monologue. "Are you trying to bore me to death?"

Julius pauses in his circuit. He's standing to my right.

"Are you in a hurry to die? If that's the case, I could draw this out for days. Maybe I'll put you in a cage on the wall, where all of your pathetic would-be-revolutionaries can watch the sand and wind scour the flesh from your bones."

"This is trial by combat, Julius. One of us has to die here. Though it wouldn't surprise me if you're such a coward you can't even look me in the face when you kill me."

Julius splutters, and takes two quick steps. He's standing just off the front of my shoulder. Almost there.

"You are a dog," he hisses. "And I'll kill you like one."

"Right here, Julius." I tilt my head back, baring my throat. I force my good eye open a crack, squinting through the blood and tears. "I don't believe you can look me in the eye while you do it."

Julius takes the final step. He's directly in front of me now, his face dark with rage. He raises his warpknife high, preparing to plunge it down into my heart.

I focus on the bright power flowing through Rory's cannon, the switch that trips when someone presses the firing stud. I reach out with my mind and flip the switch on.

The cannon blast hits Julius square in the back, knocking him off balance, stumbling straight toward me. Before he can recover, I lunge forward, and sink my warpknife straight through his heart.

52

───────────

With Julius dead, things get a little tense. Rory looks like he wants to shoot me. Castle narrows his eyes, calculating. Kass's expression is a mixture of relief and what-the-dust-just-happened. The other Guardians look from them to me and back again, hands on their warpknives.

I struggle to get to my feet. Everything hurts, and my injured legs don't want to bear my weight. Kass steps forward and puts an arm around me in support.

"Thank you," I say.

She smiles. "I guess this means you're innocent."

"I guess it does."

One of her men sprays medfoam over my wounds. I sigh as cool numbness spreads over the pain.

"I don't know how you did that, Twisty," Rory says. "But that was a spiny trick."

I raise an eyebrow at him. "Me? It was your cannon, Rory."

His face darkens. "Don't give me that dust. I did not depress the firing stud."

"Didn't you?" I laugh as his face goes from red to purple. "Relax, Rory. I'm just messing with you."

Castle looks at me with interest. "You triggered Rory's cannon? How?"

I shrug. "I've learned a few things recently. Excuse me for a second. Shadow, are you there?" I tap my com, searching the sky for the glint of a drone.

"I'm here, Twist."

"How are things down on the ground?"

"Chaotic. The Outsiders and the people in the streets are holding their own, thanks to the help of the Hubzoh, but more are dying every minute. Ianna and the Forsaken still have control of the wall, but the Guardians are trying to take it back. Things could go either way."

"Thanks, Shadow." I click off my com, and turn to face Castle. "Too many people are dying. It's time to put an end to this."

His eyes are hard. "Does that mean the rebels are surrendering?"

"No. It means you are. We've got control of the wall and the people are with us. If this war continues, all we'll be left with is a pile of corpses. A colony full of dead bodies doesn't benefit anyone."

"The IEC pays my salary. If I surrender to you, I'm out of a job. Doesn't seem like a wise career choice."

"If you don't surrender, you're going to end up in a grave beside Julius. I'd say that's a worse career choice."

Castle's hand goes to his warpknife. "Are you threatening me, pup?"

"No, Castle. That would be my job." Rust strides into view, Akona looming at his heels.

At the sight of the Hubzoh, the Guardians reach for their warpknives. All except Castle.

His mouth puckers like he wants to spit. "Steel. How dare you bring one of those things up here."

"She's not a thing and you know it." Rust halts beside me, looking both dignified and ridiculous in his antique armor. "I told you the Hubzoh were intelligent fifty years ago."

"It doesn't matter if they're intelligent or not. They're in the way of our mining operation."

Akona's carapace colors at his words, white and blue flashing over the surface. I can feel her agitation. The Guardians all take a step back.

"That statement proves you are unfit to command the Guardians." Rust draws his warpknife. "Commandant Castle, I hereby relieve you of your position. Surrender your warpknife. Guards, take him into custody."

Castle scowls. "You have no authority here."

Kass turns to me. "Who is this guy?"

"This is my friend, Rust. Better known as the legendary Captain Steel."

Her eyebrows lift. "*The* Captain Steel?"

"Once upon a time, yes." Rust inclines his head to her. "Pleased to make your acquaintance."

Kass considers him for a moment, then nods decisively.

"OK, that settles it. I'd say the greatest general in the history of this planet has seniority." She turns to her soldiers. "Take Commandant Castle into custody."

Castle glares at her, and the Guardians behind him draw their blades. Kass's crew do the same. The two forces are evenly matched: It's a deadlock.

Then Akona shuffles forward, opening and closing her warp-sharp claws. The balance tips definitively in our favor.

Castle eyes the Hubzoh with disgust and throws down his warpknife.

"Fine. Take the colony. You and your ragged band of rebels will never be able to hold it. How long do you think you have until the IEC comes down in force?"

I step forward and kick his blade away.

"That's a question for another day." I look at Kass. Her blue eyes sparkle like the promise of the dawn. "For today, this is enough."

53

We sit in a conference room in the Mesa, all of Canyon City spread out beneath our feet. The sunrise paints the sky red and gold through wall-sized windows. Looking out at all that open space doesn't make my fingers and toes tingle anymore. Maybe I've finally gotten over my fear of heights. Or maybe I'm just too tired to be scared.

The conference table is littered with half-empty cups of coffee, matté, and other stimulant drinks. It's been a long night, the latest in a string of long nights. It's like the all-night strategy session we had when we were planning Ianna's rescue from the Carlyle estate all over again, except these sessions have been going on for days, and the thing we're planning is nowhere near as simple as an extraction run.

I grind my knuckles into my dry, itchy eye. Across the table, Shadow is speaking. I realize I haven't heard a word she's said. I look around the table: Rust, Kass and Ianna are nodding over their mugs. Knott's head is down on her arm, her eyes closed. A thin string of drool connects the corner of her mouth to the table.

"Let's call it a night," I interrupt. "Get some rest. We can pick up here tomorrow."

Bleary eyes turn toward me. I can see their sluggish minds struggling to process my words.

One by one, they get it and push tiredly to their feet.

Rust is first out the door, staggering away without a backward glance. The face of Canyon City's new Commandant is drawn and thin, his many years apparent in the deep ravines running across his forehead. He and Kass have been the key to keeping the Guardians in line. Without their authority, we'd probably still be fighting.

Kass stops beside me, yawning and stretching. "He's amazing. No wonder he's such a legend."

"I don't know how he does it. If I'm still breathing at his age, it'll be a miracle," I agree.

I look down, shuffling my feet awkwardly. There are so many things I need to say to Kass. So many bridges burned. I don't know if they can ever be repaired, but I guess you've got to start somewhere.

"I'm sorry I didn't tell you," I say. "About my dad and my sister. The Outsiders. About, well … everything."

She turns her eyes toward the window, taking in the brightening sky.

"I understand why you couldn't tell me," she says finally, "but that doesn't make it hurt any less. You could have trusted me, Twist. I wouldn't have betrayed you."

"I hoped you wouldn't, but I couldn't be sure. You did grow up in Sunrise. And there were more people at risk than just me. I couldn't gamble with their lives, I'm sorry. I'll try to do better next time."

"That's all we can do isn't it? Try to do better next time?"

"Yeah, I guess it is."

She searches my face, and I can see she wants to say more. My stomach knots, anticipating and dreading her words. There are kilometers of underground tunnels here. Thoughts and feelings that have never seen the light of day. Instead, she presses her lips together and nods.

"Goodnight, Twist."

"Goodnight, Kass."

I watch her walk away, admiring her straight spine and strong, lean back, the bouncing curl of her hair. Wondering if I'll ever touch that hair again.

"Don't you mean, good morning?" In contrast with the rest of us, Ianna's eyes are still bright. She's been fantastic with supply train logistics during the transition period, calculating how to keep the people of Canyon City fed while we work on making the colony self-sustaining. I can practically see her mind clicking the puzzle pieces together.

It must be the magic of youth. Either that or the Forsaken biotech she's got implanted in her skull.

But I'd rather not think about that. Who or what my sister is becoming is a problem for another day. Right now, I'm just glad she's here.

"I guess you could go either way. " I reach out and ruffle her hair. Ianna squirms away like she always has. I smile, glad to see my sister's not all grown up quite yet.

"Get some sleep," I order. "Don't stay up working on spreadsheets all day."

"But I like spreadsheets!"

"Sleep. Go. Now."

"Fine. I guess I can't argue with the Governor." She sticks her tongue out at me and skips through the door.

I sigh and rub the back of my neck. Governor. I still can't believe that's me. I don't want the title, but our little council decided it was important to have a figurehead people could look up to. And after all that "Cyclops" nonsense, I've become some kind of myth in Canyon City. The others say if anyone can hold our budding independent colony together, it's me. So I guess I'm stuck with the title for now.

Shadow slips up beside me. "Should we wake Knott?"

I consider the big tank. Her cheek is smashed flat on the tabletop, but other than that, she looks pretty comfortable.

"Nah, let her sleep. She gets grumpy if you wake her."

Shadow chuckles and doesn't say anything else as the bright disk of the sun finally crests the lip of the canyon, falling warm on our faces.

"Any sign of Grab?" I ask.

Shadow's face sobers.

"No. His body is definitely dead. Someone pulled the plug on him during the battle. They must have figure out he was helping us. If he managed to achieve his dream of becoming an AI and upload his consciousness, I haven't been able to find him. But I haven't had much time to look, honestly. My team is working on a lot of high priority things."

"I understand. Keep looking."

"I will."

A sad silence falls now, as we both wonder if our friend is truly gone this time. Grab has survived so much, I figured he was indestructible. I thought it was just a matter of time before he uploaded. I hope he's still out there, somewhere.

Shadow sighs.

"Rory escaped from his cell last night. He and Ghengis were seen slipping out into the scablands."

I grind my teeth. Now I'm glad Knott's asleep; she'd be furious.

"I know killing people is wrong, but a part of me really wishes Knott just finished off Ghengis when she had the chance," I say.

"She left him secured and in custody. He was going to answer for his crimes. Someone let him go."

"Which means we've got traitors in our midst."

"We've probably got several," she agrees. "We don't have enough people to keep order without using the Guardians, and a lot of them are still loyal to the IEC. I'll be interviewing them all individually and weeding out the bad ones, but it's going to take time."

"Do you think they'll come back?"

"No, I think Rory and Ghengis will head for one of the other colonies. If I had to guess, I'd say they'll head for White Rock, that's where the spaceport is, and IEC headquarters."

My jaw relaxes a fraction. White Rock is thousands of kilometers away.

"Hopefully, that means Rory and Ghengis are someone else's problem now," I say.

"Hopefully."

"I don't know what I'm doing," I admit softly.

"None of us do. We've got an entire colony to run now. There are hundreds of things that need to be dealt with that are beyond our experience."

"But I'm the governor. The people look at me like I'm some kind of hero. It's not right."

"No man is a hero to himself," Jmini breaks in, projecting his voice so Shadow can hear him too. "Ray Bradbury once wrote that."

"Are you kidding?" I say. "What about Heda Dustorm or Captain Steel?"

"Does Rust seem like he considers himself a hero?"

"Well, no, but when he was younger…"

"Jmini's right," Shadow says. "Other people make you a hero. To yourself, you're always just a person, muddling through and trying to do the right thing. Taking life one day at a time."

"So you're saying it never gets any easier? That's not very comforting."

"It's life, Twist. It's not supposed to be comforting. That's what your friends are for." Shadow puts her arms around my waist and squeezes.

After a moment, I return the hug. I keep my arm around her shoulders and we stand there, leaning against each other.

"Thousands of people aren't working under the thumb of the IEC any longer. If they want to call you a hero for that, you should let them. People choose their heroes. Heroes don't choose themselves."

"But…"

She puts a finger over my lips. "Yes, there's still a lot of work to do. There always will be. But we did an amazing thing, Twist. Canyon City is free. We ended generations of misery. Shut up and let yourself enjoy that for a minute."

Sometimes you have to know when to listen to your friends. So I do.

I lean against Shadow, the warmth of the rising sun matched by the warmth of our friendship. Below, the golden rays creep down the spires of Canyon City, bringing light to thousands of people. Thousands of people who are now free. They stumble out into the dusty streets and raise their faces in hope, basking in the light of a new day.

END of CYCLE ONE

Dear Reader,

Before you go back to your regularly scheduled life, I'd like to ask a quick favor.

The importance of reviews in today's publishing industry cannot be overstressed. We all look at what others have to say before trying something new, it's just human nature. So if you enjoyed PEAK, and Cycle One, I would be very grateful if you took a moment to leave a short review so that others can find this story and enjoy it as well. Even just a couple of words would really mean lot. This handy universal link will take you to most online booksellers. https://books2read.com/u/megK8g

Thank you!

- J.S.

AFTERWORD

Well, we've reached the end of Cycle One of The Crimson Dust Cycle. I hope you've enjoyed the journey as much as I have. Twist, Shadow, Knott, Kass, Ianna, Rust, and the rest of the crew have carved a permanent home in my heart and mind. It's a place full of friendship and adventure that I'll carry with me always. I hope you will too.

I'm hard at work on Cycle Two of The Crimson Dust Cycle, which is forthcoming in Fall 2020. A whole new arc of adventures awaits. I look forward to sharing it with you. To stay informed of the release dates and for access to exclusive deals, become part of my Reader's Group at www.arquinworlds.com.

Thank you so much for reading. We are going great places together, you and I.

Until next time,
Keep dreaming.
- J.S. Arquin. April, 2020

ABOUT THE AUTHOR

J.S. Arquin lives in his own worlds. At least, that's what his teachers always told him when they caught him reading books inside his desk instead of paying attention in class.

These days, he fills those worlds with stories of fantastic places & extraordinary people, which he dutifully shares with his readers. He still lives inside them. He is aware that some people claim there is a "real world" out there.

J.S. remains unconvinced.

When not writing, he spends his time narrating audiobooks, working on his podcast, The Overcast, drinking too much caffeine, playing board games and ping pong, and riding his bicycle in the rain.

He is hard at work on the next book in The Crimson Dust Cycle.

Explore his worlds and sign up for his exclusive reader group at www.arquinworlds.com

****

Found a typo? This book has been through several rounds of editing and proofing, but mistakes still happen. Please inform us of any errors you find so that we can fix them for the next edition. email: js@arquinworlds.com

ALSO BY J.S. ARQUIN

ASCENT: Book One of The Crimson Dust Cycle

SLIDE: Book Two of The Crimson Dust Cycle

PEAK: Book Three of the Crimson Dust Cycle

TWIST: A Crimson Dust Cycle Prequel

www.ingramcontent.com/pod-product-compliance
Lightning Source LLC
Chambersburg PA
CBHW050513190726
48284CB00003B/800